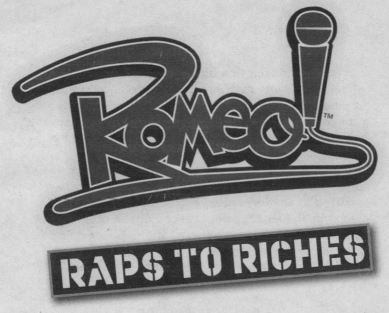

RAPS TO RICHES

By Holly Kowitt

Created by Tom Lynch

SCHOLASTIC INC.

New York   Toronto   London   Auckland   Sydney
Mexico City   New Dehli   Hong Kong   Buenos Aires

No part of this work may be reproduced in whole or in part, stored in a retrieval system, or trans-mitted in any form or by any means, electronic, mechanical, photocopying, recording, or otherwise, without written permission of the publisher. For information regarding permission, write to Scho-lastic Inc., Attention: Permissions Department, 557 Broadway, New York, NY 10012.

ISBN 0-439-79667-9

© 2006. Nickelodeon, Romeo, and all related titles, logos and characters are trademarks of Viacom International Inc.

Published by Scholastic Inc.
SCHOLASTIC and associated logos are trademarks and/or registered trademarks of Scholastic Inc.

12 11 10 9 8 7 6 5 4 3 2 1   6 7 8 9 10/0

Printed in the U.S.A.
First printing, January 2006

CHAPTER 1

MYSTERY GIRL

All the students in freshman English class were totally focused on the test papers in front of them — except for Romeo Miller. He sat at his desk, staring dreamily at Peyton Cruz. She was writing swiftly, unaware of Romeo's gaze.

Ever since Peyton had borrowed his eraser on the first day of class, Romeo had been unable to take his eyes off her. Besides being cute, she was kind, smart, funny, and full of surprises. He loved seeing the creative outfits she put together, like a tuxedo shirt with red overalls, or a sundress with a silk flower in her hair.

When the teacher called his name for the first time while taking attendance, Peyton had taken notice of him. "Your name is Romeo? As in *Romeo and Juliet*?"

she asked, her brown eyes shining. "That's one of my favorite plays. What a great love story."

Romeo was impressed. She liked Shakespeare, but she was also a jock. He'd seen her in the school yard in a striped soccer uniform, kicking a winning goal. Peyton had other interests, too, including music. She played flute in the school jazz band, and he often saw her carrying around a little black case.

Ro also liked that she was curious about him. On their walks home from school, Peyton had asked him about being part of a large family, his budding music career, and tryouts for the basketball team. She seemed genuinely interested.

She's so beautiful, he thought, gazing at her dark eyes which were totally focused on the paper in front of her. Her black hair contrasted with her colorful blue, green, and red halter top. A silver spiral choker and silver hoop earrings sparkled against her light brown skin.

The bell rang, tearing Romeo out of his trance. He rushed to fill in the last few answers and tossed the paper on Ms. Chang's desk. Stuffing his books into his black-and-silver backpack, he raced out of the classroom, hoping to catch Peyton at her locker.

Bolting down the hall, he stopped a few feet from Peyton's locker and resumed his usual unhurried stroll. *Be cool*, he told himself. Peyton was applying lip gloss in front of a small mirror inside her locker.

The door was decorated with stickers shaped like hearts and stars. Also hanging inside the locker were a postcard from Paris, a soccer pennant, and posters of her favorite R&B singers.

"Hey, Peyton," he said, as if he just happened to notice her.

"Hi, Romeo," said Peyton.

"Did you have a chance to listen to the CD I gave you?" asked Romeo, trying to sound casual.

Romeo had given her a compilation of songs by his band, the Romeo Show. The group was made up of Romeo's brothers and sister: Jodi, Louis, and Gary. Lately they'd been getting a lot of local attention for their playful raps and silky vocals.

As the group's lead rapper, Ro was proud of how far they'd come. Lately, even their dad, Percy —

a well-known record producer — had to admit they sounded pretty tight. The Miller kids knew they wouldn't get an easy "in" to the music biz from their father, though. Percy Miller wanted the kids to make it on their own.

"Your music is fantastic," said Peyton, handing the disk back to him. "The rhymes really knocked me out."

Ro was totally stoked, but reminded himself to tone it down. "Yeah?" he said, grinning. "Cool."

Peyton looked at Romeo thoughtfully. "I don't know how you do it. My favorite song is 'Mystery Girl,'" she said, playing with her hair ornament.

Romeo nodded happily. That song was one of his favorites, too. "So who is the Mystery Girl?" Peyton asked playfully, her silver earrings bobbing up and down.

Romeo smiled. "Peyton, if I told you who the Mystery Girl was . . . it wouldn't be a mystery." He broke off, noticing something odd. In front of his best friend Louis's locker was a guy in a strange wire-mesh mask, with a white jacket and sword, pulling stuff out.

Someone was breaking into Lou's locker!

Ro turned back to Peyton. "I'll catch up with you later," he said, and slowly approached the masked man. "Yo, you. With the face. That's my brother's locker. So just shut the door and walk away." With both index fingers, Romeo pointed away from the locker.

Suddenly, Romeo had a sword pressed against his chest. The masked man had him pinned to the locker. "Whoa!" cried Romeo, dropping his backpack.

With a dramatic motion, the swordsman pulled off his mask — it was Louis! "What do you think?" he asked, shaking out his spiky blond hair.

"Scary," said Ro, catching his breath. "Very scary," Romeo repeated. What was Louis up to?

Louis explained that McDaniel, their Seattle high school, had started a fencing club. Beginners were welcome, so why not? Ro looked dubious. "So, this is, like, sword fights and stuff?" Ro asked. Louis went into a ninja warrior routine, swinging the foil around the hallway.

"Prepare to die, scoundrel!" Lou shouted in a pirate voice, and set himself to lunge forward. Ro ducked, and Louis's foil got stuck in one of the locker vents. He dropped his warrior stance and struggled to dislodge it.

He tugged at the sword, grunting as he tried to wiggle it loose. When it finally came free, Louis sprang backward and landed flat on his rear end. Sprawled on the floor, he looked up at his brother. Ro shook his head.

"Dawg, you're my boy," said Ro. "I didn't say anything when you took banjo lessons. And the time you tried to start a trend by wearing your underwear on the outside of your pants, I kept my mouth shut."

Romeo had always watched over Louis, even though his best friend was a year older than him. Lou was good-natured, goofy, and sometimes a little naive. Since he started living with the Millers a few years back, Louis had become a crucial part of the mix. He was like a brother to Romeo, and together Lou and Ro were the ultimate partners in crime.

In the past few years, they'd grown especially close. Together they'd played music, sports, and pranks. They'd shared secrets, family crises, disappointments, victories, and adjoining bunk beds. Romeo felt free to give his brother advice, even when he didn't ask for it.

Louis stood up and rubbed his backside. "So what's your point?" he asked irritably. He flexed the sword to make sure it wasn't damaged. Again, he thrust the sword at Romeo.

"This is lame," said Ro, pointing to Louis's clunky white jacket. "I mean, what kind of kid other than you is interested in fencing?"

At that moment, Peyton walked by, dressed in full fencing attire. She gave Louis a cute wave as she passed. Louis turned to Romeo and threw his arm around him. "I guess a kid like Peyton," he said, with a sly smile.

Romeo admitted defeat. "Touché," he said, watching Peyton as she disappeared into the cafeteria.

Louis had definitely won this round.

CHAPTER 2

SCHOOL DAZE

Romeo's face was pressed against the school cafeteria window. Inside, the fencers were practicing, crossing swords in a blizzard of metal. One fencer was working her opponent with astonishing skill, leaping and parrying with the elegance of a ballerina.

Finally, the fencer removed her mask. It was Peyton, shaking out her black curls.

"Excuse me?" A voice woke Romeo from his trance, and he spun around quickly. Mr. Frink, his teacher, was standing in front of him. "Mr. Miller, you know there's no loitering after four o'clock," he said, frowning and looking at his watch.

Romeo held up a red pail filled with cleaning supplies. "I'm not loitering," he explained, dangling the pail. "I'm just getting ready to clean my locker." His eyes wandered to the window again.

Mr. Frink gave Ro a look, knowing there was more to the story. He motioned toward the cafeteria. "You seem pretty interested in the fencing club," he observed.

"No!" said Romeo, a little too loudly. "I'm not. I'm just getting ready to clean my . . ." His voice trailed off. He watched Peyton step out of the cafeteria to get a drink at the water fountain. Nodding hello at Romeo and Mr. Frink, she headed back to the cafeteria.

Ro's face broke out into a goofy grin as he watched her. Man, she was cute. Even in her white fencing uniform, she had a spunky charm that belonged to no one else. Mr. Frink looked at Peyton, and then at Romeo. He realized why Romeo wanted to linger after school.

"Romeo?" he said, in a voice that was deadly serious. "You have my permission to stay and clean your locker," he said. Ro barely heard him. Mr. Frink walked away from Romeo, shaking his head and smiling to himself.

Back at Romeo's house, his little brother, Gary, approached his shiny new car, caressing the roof as he walked beside it. "Ah, my sweet ride," he said, as he opened the door. At eight years old, he was the youngest kid in the neighborhood to own a car. He had won it in a radio call-in contest, beating out his seventeen-year-old sister Jodi.

The radio station, K-HYPE, hadn't realized he was only in second grade. Still, he'd won it fair and square, and the car belonged to him. In the driver's seat, he reached to turn on the radio.

Darn! His arm still didn't reach.

He tried again, but fell short of the dashboard by several inches. Reaching down to adjust the seat, his hand collided with a box of Fiber Thin crackers. *What's this?* he thought. Taking a deep breath, he pulled out the mileage log.

Being a natural businessman, Gary had set up a system of car rules. Anyone who wanted to use it had to request permission, and write down their mileage. He was finicky about keeping records.

The last entry was Thursday the seventh: seven miles to the shoe emporium. This brought the total to 235 miles, he calculated. But the odometer read 239. What?

Someone had helped themselves to a four-mile joyride!

Gary looked at the cracker box in disgust. Slamming the mileage log shut, he stormed out of the car and into the house. Whoever did it was going to pay, big-time.

Inside, Romeo's stepmom, Angeline, sat at the drawing board in her home office. As a busy architect, she often had deadlines. Still, the Miller kids always came to talk to her when they had a problem, and she always took the time to listen.

Since she'd married their father almost a year ago, Angeline had become a mainstay of the Miller family. Everyone depended on her patience, humor, and common sense. When their father was away on his frequent business trips, she held the household together.

Besides her statuesque beauty and warm brown eyes, Angeline was also fun. Having lost their own mother years ago, the Miller kids were grateful to have such a cool stepmom.

Now Angeline was bent over her drawing board, listening to Jodi chatter about her new crush. With her long black hair and brown velour warm-up suit, Angeline looked as youthful as her stepdaughter, a senior in high school.

"He does the cutest thing with his eyebrows whenever he yawns," Jodi gushed. "And his name . . . he has the cutest name." Jodi couldn't wait long enough for Angeline to respond. "Ralston," she announced. "Isn't that cute?" She squealed and put her hands on her hips.

"The cutest," Angeline assured her, smiling to herself. She could tell Jodi was about to ask permission for something.

"So, I know it's a school night," Jodi began tentatively. "But he wanted to take me out for, like, an hour." Jodi bit her lip, afraid to look at Angeline.

Amazingly, Angeline agreed. "As long as you do your homework, it's alright with me," she said with a shrug. Jodi hugged herself with joy. *Yessss!*

Her happy dance was cut short when they heard

the kitchen door slam. A furious Gary stomped into the room. He stopped, folded his arms across his chest, and glared at Jodi. Angeline looked from Gary to Jodi. "What's wrong?" she asked.

"Fiber Thins!" Gary shouted. "That's what's wrong." Jodi grabbed the box he held, turning her back on Gary.

"Where'd you find these?" she asked, scared to hear the answer.

"Oh, you know . . . IN MY CAR, which you've obviously been driving," said Gary, fuming. Jodi started to deny it, but Gary continued. "You wanna drive my car, you know you're supposed to put in a request twenty-four hours beforehand. IN WRITING!" he shouted.

Jodi fled the room, and Gary looked up at Angeline. "I think I'll let you two sort this out," she said, bending over her table. *Okay,* Gary said to himself.

But he knew that in the future, he wouldn't be taken advantage of again.

Back at school, Romeo halfheartedly wiped his locker with a paper towel. As he cleaned, he kept an eye on the door of the cafeteria, where the fencing club was wrapping up. Romeo watched Lou and Peyton talking, trying to read their lips from a distance. No luck — he couldn't hear what they were saying.

Then he saw Louis unzipping the back of Peyton's white fencing vest. Peyton unzipped Louis. They stood in their gym clothes, talking. Romeo flinched, watching Peyton finally walk away. Louis joined him at his locker.

"What are you doing here so late?" asked Lou, eyeing his bucket of supplies.

"Cleaning my locker," replied Romeo. "Like I always say: clean locker, clear mind," said Romeo, bunching up a paper towel.

"You've never said that," Lou said, looking skeptical. "Your locker always looks like a toxic waste dump."

"Well, maybe not out loud," said Ro, defensively. Lou handed him the cleanser and Ro squirted it. Nothing.

"You have to turn the nozzle," Lou pointed out, twisting it for him. Ro squirted, and the spray went all over his face.

"Awwwwwwww," Ro groaned, while Louis laughed. He took the bottle away so Ro could wipe his face.

"So," Ro began, with careful nonchalance. "Fencing practice over?"

Louis nodded, and babbled on about the people on the team. "Did you know Jerry Steckler's brother only has four fingers?" he asked.

"That's, um, fascinating," said Romeo. "So . . . did you talk to Peyton at all?" he asked, trying to sound offhand.

"Yeah," said Louis. "She's cool." He started to explain what she'd said about Jerry Steckler's brother.

"Did she say anything about me?" Romeo asked impatiently. Louis thought about it for a moment and shook his head. Romeo's face fell.

"Ro, is this weirding you out? You know, me hanging out with Peyton and all?" Lou asked. It seemed like Ro was bothered about something.

Romeo stood up straighter. "Hey, no worries, bro," he said, chuckling. "You two wanna play Zorro," he said, swishing an imaginary sword, "it's alright with me."

Lou looked at his brother's cleaning supplies and shook his head. Somehow, he wasn't convinced. . . .

CHAPTER 3

BREAKING THE RULES

Angeline set down a clothes hamper in front of the boys' bedroom. She called to Gary to collect the dirty laundry off the floor. The bedroom — shared by Romeo, Lou, and Gary — was always messy, but the boys loved it.

Cluttered with sports equipment, books, and toys, it was cozy and comfortable. The walls were lined with old street signs, music posters, and a basketball hoop. It was big enough to hold Ro's CDs, Louis's model rockets, and Gary's stuffed animal collection.

Angeline showed up at the door again. "Gary? The laundry?" she reminded him.

Gary barely looked up at her. "I got it, I got it," he said.

He was sitting on his bed, looking at the mileage

log. He added it up again and got the same result. Jodi had *definitely* used the car. Reluctantly, he pulled some tube socks off the floor.

As he stuffed them in the hamper, Gary heard his sister come up the stairs, talking on the cordless phone. "But, Ralston . . ." she pleaded. "I want to see you, too." Thinking quickly, Gary jumped into the hamper. He wanted to overhear her conversation.

"We don't need to cancel 'cuz your dad won't let you use his car," Jodi continued. "I'll pick you up. But it has to be after my little brother goes to sleep." She whispered the last sentence.

Under a pile of clothes, Gary strained to hear more. "*Why?*" repeated Jodi into the phone. "It's hard to explain," she said. "How's 9:15? . . . Great, see you then." Jodi pounded the hamper in delight. She whistled as she skipped down the hall to her room.

Throwing open her closet, Jodi pondered clothing options. Her yellow silk tank seemed too dressy, but her pink polo shirt didn't seem dressy enough. She felt a twinge of guilt about the car. But it's not like Gary would be using it anyway, she thought.

It isn't fair, thought Jodi. *Gary can't even drive!*

But he was very fussy about other people using the car, always going on about his stupid mileage log. I *should have won that radio contest,* thought Jodi.

After all, *she* was the one who'd told him about the contest in the first place. She'd promised to take him to the movies, but canceled their outing to stay home and enter the contest. When he'd found out why she canceled, he'd dialed into the radio station himself.

Who would have ever guessed he'd win?

Jodi looked at her closet again. Maybe the white halter top . . .

Climbing out of the basket, Gary shook off a pair of briefs that stuck to his cornrows. Thinking about Jodi sneaking off with his car made him furious. He remembered the box of Fiber Thins left on the floor. Why did she think she could use it whenever she wanted?

He had created the rules for a reason. He didn't want his family to think the car belonged to the adults. In only eight more years, he'd be able to drive himself. He had to keep the car in good shape.

This time, he was going to teach her a lesson.

Her date with Ralston was going to have a few surprises. *Fasten your seat belts,* he thought with a smile. *It's going to be a bumpy ride.* . . .

Slumped at the kitchen table, Louis crumpled up another piece of paper. He tried to toss it behind him, onto a pile of previously discarded wads. Instead, it landed on Angeline's drafting table.

"Homework trouble?" she asked, sympathetically.

"I'm supposed to write an ode," said Louis, wrinkling up his forehead. He said it as though he were announcing a lengthy prison sentence. Angeline reached for the crumpled piece of paper and asked if she could take a look.

Smoothing out the paper, she read the title aloud. "'Ode to a Beautiful Lady,'" she said. "Who's the beautiful lady?" she asked. "Someone in your class?"

"Sandy," said Louis. Angeline looked blank. "Mrs. Guthrie's golden retriever," he explained. Angeline started to laugh, then cleared her throat and tried to look serious as she read the rest of the poem aloud.

"When I run my fingers through your hair,/I am more aware /Of how you make my day golden/Like the grass that we rolled in." Lou looked embarrassed. Angeline put her arm around him. "C'mon, it's not so bad. . . ."

After giving him a squeeze, Angeline went back to her drafting table. Louis sank back in his chair, looking at his notebook. He tried to think of more things to write about Sandy from his week of dog-sitting. Something about tick baths? Worm pills?

Lou chewed on his pen. He just wasn't feeling inspired right now.

"You have a lovely coat, and a soft brown throat. . . ." he wrote. This poetry stuff was hard. He shook his head and crumpled up another piece of paper.

The phone rang, and Angeline leaped for it. Romeo burst through the door, beating her to it. He was shiny with sweat, and he carried a basketball. He dropped the ball to pick up the receiver. Peyton's voice on the other end surprised him.

"Hello, Romeo," she said. *Wow*, thought Ro. He didn't even know Peyton knew his number. He was thrilled.

"Ho, ho, hey, Peyton. What's going on?" he

asked. While he talked, he glanced around the room for a chair he could settle into. "I was just outside, working on my jump shot," he said, picking up the ball. "You know, the secret is in the follow-through," he said. "So, what's up?"

"Actually, I called to speak to Louis," said Peyton.

Louis? Romeo felt stung. "Huh? Louis?" he said. "Yeah, he's right here."

Grudgingly, he handed the phone to his brother. Lou took the receiver and started chatting easily. "Oh, hey, what's going on?" Louis asked. "C'mon, it was crazy. You only beat me by one point!"

Listening to Louis's responses, Romeo tried to construct Peyton's side of the conversation. They talked about fencing practice, fencing partners. . . . Romeo strained to hear more. Louis continued to talk and laugh, taking the phone into the next room.

Romeo put down his basketball. He was no longer in the mood to play.

CHAPTER 4

DATE WITH DISASTER

The boys' bedroom was dark when Jodi tiptoed in. After a quick look to make sure Gary was asleep, she carefully lifted the car key. It was on a hook next to the headboard, dangling from a plastic dinosaur keychain.

Jodi always smiled when she saw the dinosaur. *That's what happens when an eight-year-old has his own car*, she thought. Seeing her brother deep in slumber, she fought the urge to tousle his hair.

He looked so sweet lying there, his braids tucked inside an animal print do-rag. Thinking about how she'd made him so upset today made her wince. Now she felt guilty about sneaking off with the car. *I'll never use it again without his permission*, Jodi promised silently.

After tonight, that is. She simply had to see Ralston tonight or she'd go crazy. The vibe between them had been building all week, but she'd been too busy with student council, band rehearsal, and studying. It was time for their first real date.

She remembered the first time she'd spotted Ralston. It had been at drama club. They were rehearsing *Julius Caesar*, and Ralston was playing Brutus. Even dressed as a Roman senator, he was handsome. It wasn't every guy who looked good in a toga.

But most of all, she enjoyed talking to him. He spoke about museum exhibits and plays he'd attended. Not like some guys, she thought, who only wanted to talk about their latest football game. She thought they had a lot in common.

How lucky for her that Angeline had been home today! Her father might not have agreed to her going out on a school night. Jodi felt a flash of gratitude toward her stepmother. Angeline seemed genuinely happy that Jodi had met someone nice.

Ang had even lent Jodi her red-and-silver choker for the evening. "Just this once," she said, fastening the delicate chain around Jodi's neck. The necklace went perfectly with the dazzling white halter top she wore with a red skirt.

Jodi snuck one more look at herself in the mirror. Perfection!

"I'll be home by ten-thirty," she called out to Angeline. That should be enough time to go to the drive-in diner, drink milk shakes, and let Ralston know how much she liked him. She had been rehearsing the words she'd say all day.

As soon as Gary heard the front door slam, he bolted up in bed. He grabbed a teddy bear wearing a do-rag and stuffed some pillows under the quilt. *Pretty convincing*, thought Gary. It looked like he was in bed, sleeping.

He was fully clothed under his blanket, so all he had to do was pull on his sneakers. Closing his bedroom door, he tiptoed downstairs. He had to move fast.

Meanwhile, Ro tried to concentrate on his math homework. Trying to calculate the area of a trapezoid was hard enough, but with Louis blabbing on the phone to Peyton in the hall, it was next to impossible.

"Crazy, huh?" Louis was saying. " What? You did not." After a pause, he said, "Oh, you do not." Another pause, and then, "You will not."

Fascinating conversation, Romeo said to himself. He shifted in his chair. More laughter drifted out into the kitchen.

Now Louis was almost screaming. "Get *out*!" he shouted. "You're killin' me!" He collapsed into laughter, and Ro heard him pound his feet on the floor. Angeline had to step over him to get back into the kitchen.

When Ang walked through the door, Ro slammed down his textbook.

His stepmother looked at him quizzically. "I'm trying to focus on my work," Romeo protested.

Louis burst into laughter again. "You did not. . . ." his brother said into the phone. "Oh, you are *so* gonna pay for this. . . ."

Ro grabbed his textbook and pencil, leaving the room noisily. He kicked a toy race car out of the way. Louis was saying to Peyton, "Oh, man, that's hilarious!"

After he snatched his book and left the house,

he let the door slam loudly. Angeline looked after him, concerned. It wasn't like Ro to lose his temper over a loud phone call.

What was going on?

Across town, Jodi looked at Ralston in the car seat next to her. *What a cutie*, she thought, eyeing his dark curly hair and broad shoulders. He looked handsome in a dark blue polo shirt, and she could smell the musky scent of his aftershave. She smiled at him, and he smiled back.

Looking at him, she reflected that his polo shirt was buttoned up a bit high. For a guy, he seemed fussy about his appearance. She had caught him checking his hair in the mirror, but she didn't mind. It showed their date was important to him.

"This place is great," said Ralston, looking around at the 1950s-style drive-in diner she'd suggested. All the waiters were dressed as old-fashioned carhops, in orange shirts and pedal pushers. On the windshield, they could see a reflection of the neon MALT SHOP sign.

"You know, Ralston, I was really happy when

you called," said Jodi, dipping a french fry into a pool of ketchup.

"Indeed," said Ralston, taking a sip of his soda. "I don't know why it took me so long."

Jody straightened her necklace. "Must be hard being a guy sometimes," she reflected. "You know, having to open up and ask a girl out." Outside the window, an orange carhop skated by.

"Indeed," he said. "But it'd be harder not to ask a girl, when the girl is you," Ralston said, smiling. He smoothed back his hair, checking the mirror again.

So far, this date was off to a good start, Jodi thought.

"Ah, rats," he said, shaking his head. "Got ketchup on my jeans." Jodi saw that he had dropped a French fry. "These are vintage," he explained, nervously rubbing the stain with a napkin.

"Not that I'm into possessions," he assured her, clearing his throat. He offered to go grab some more napkins.

"Hurry back!" she called out, as he left the car and disappeared into the malt shop.

Taking advantage of his absence, she slipped a

breath strip into her mouth. The peppermint taste exploded on her tongue. She tilted the rearview mirror to check on her lipstick. Looking in the mirror, she saw Gary. GARY???

She looked again. It *was* Gary!

"Agggggghhhhhhhh!" she screamed. She turned around, gasping for breath. "Gary!" she cried. "What are you doing here?" They were face-to-face.

"Shouldn't I be asking you that?" he said. He was sprawled out in the backseat, legs crossed. She couldn't believe her eyes.

"You scared the . . ." Jodi began, still shaking. "Are you crazy?"

Gary shook his head. "Jodi, Jodi, Jodi," he began. "I knew you'd been lying to me . . . but for *this* dude?" He shook his head some more, and looked up at the ceiling. "I just thought he'd be . . . cooler," said Gary.

In spite of herself, Jodi asked what he meant. Gary started counting on his fingers.

"Well, he likes to say the word indeed a lot," pointed out Gary. "Not to mention the perfume he's wearing."

Jodi gritted her teeth. "It's called aftershave,"

she said. She looked out the window frantically. Ralston would be back any moment.

"They should call it poison," said Gary. "Freddy just shriveled up and died," he said, pointing to his shirt.

"Who's Freddy?" asked Jodi, afraid to find out.

"Freddy's the hair in my armpit," he said.

"You named it?" said Jodi, disgusted.

"Don't change the subject," said Gary.

Jodi started to plead with him. "Look, Gary, I'm sorry I lied to you," she said. "It won't happen again, I promise." Jodi checked the window again to see if Ralston was coming.

What was she going to do when Ralston came back? Tell him her brother had hijacked their date because she had taken the car without asking? This was turning into a nightmare!

"Gary, I really like this guy," said Jodi, her heart pounding. "Get back down in the seat — please! He'll be here any minute." She smoothed out her skirt and looked around nervously.

Gary was in no hurry, though. He sniffed the air, remarking, "I can smell him. He's around." Jodi looked up and saw Ralston approach the car. Her heart sank.

"Enjoy your evening," Gary said sweetly. He ducked behind the seat, just as Ralston reentered with a fistful of napkins.

"Hey, that was fast," she said, dismayed to see him.

"Indeed," said Ralston. "Now, where were we?"

Jodi winced. How was she going to get through the rest of the evening?

CHAPTER 5

OUR LITTLE SECRET

Back at the house, Romeo slouched as he walked up the stairs to his bedroom. He glanced at the phone in the hallway, noting the green "in use" light was still on. Romeo felt another flash of annoyance toward Louis.

He'd been on the phone with Peyton for over an hour.

What were they talking about? Ro was itching to pick up the phone. Looking around to make sure he was alone, he stepped up to the table where the phone sat. Delicately, he picked up the receiver.

He caught the last half of Peyton's sentence: ". . . okay, so just remember, we can't tell anyone about this," she said in a low voice.

"Absolutely," agreed Louis. "It'll be our little secret."

Romeo's heart was pounding in his chest, but he remained silent.

"Especially not Romeo," said Peyton. Ro flinched when he heard his name. What was that about?

Louis reassured her. "Don't worry, he'll freak out when he finds out, but he won't hear it from me. . . ." Freak out? He was already freaking out! Romeo was still shaking when he replaced the receiver. His worst fears had come true.

Now he knew there was something going on between Louis and Peyton. He had heard it with his own ears! They were keeping their relationship secret from everyone, including him. *Especially* him.

When had it started? Maybe it had happened on that first day of fencing practice. He should have told Louis to leave Peyton alone. Instead, he had said to his brother, "If you two wanna play Zorro, it's alright with me."

What was he thinking?

Romeo couldn't shake the image of Louis and

Peyton unzipping each other's fencing vests. He remembered how they had laughed together during practice. Louis had never displayed any interest in fencing before.

So why had he suddenly turned into one of the Three Musketeers?

Romeo's imagination took flight. He could see it all now. Louis had only joined the fencing club so he could be near Peyton. Romeo had talked about her so much that he had gotten Louis interested. So Louis had decided to go after Peyton himself, when Romeo wasn't around.

Looking back on his history with Louis, Romeo recalled when his friend had first come to live with the Millers. He had been a shy kid then. But the warm and loving Miller household had been good for Louis, and he'd gotten more confident.

Too confident, as far as Romeo was concerned.

Romeo tore downstairs and fled to the garage, which had been converted into a rehearsal studio. With its music posters, cast-off furniture, and old 45 records mounted on the wall, it was the perfect place to hang out and think. Romeo sank into a lime-green beanbag chair.

Even when he wasn't practicing, the garage was a haven from the hectic household. Being in this room with his stacks of CDs, keyboard, and turntable, always made Romeo feel better. He liked having his music around him.

Romeo picked up his rhyme book, wondering if he could find inspiration in the situation. Heartbreak and betrayal were great subjects for songs. Romeo stared at the blank page, chewing his pen. Nothing.

He glanced at the phone they kept on an old coffee table. The light was still on.

Sighing, Romeo put the book down. He went over to the console and cued up the track to "Mystery Girl," the song Peyton said was her favorite.

He stood up and started singing furiously.

"I know we can get through
My mystery girl
It's crazy, we've been together three days
I need you in my life, girl, don't go away

Who's gonna take you for walks to school?
I know we can get through
My mystery girl. . . ."

As he sang, he watched himself in the mirror. He rocked back and forth to the music, feeling the lyrics with new intensity. Out of the corner of his eye, he watched the green phone light. Still on.

He repeated the chorus, his eyes fixed on the phone. He tried out some new moves, rolling his body to the beat. Eyes still on the phone. With his hand gestures, he acted out the song, word for word. But his eyes never left the phone. In spite of that, his moves looked good . . . too bad no one was around for his heartfelt performance.

Suddenly, the light stopped flashing. Louis was finally off the phone! Romeo stormed out of the garage, cutting off the last notes of "Mystery Girl." Now he could have it out with his brother about Peyton.

Breathing hard, he raced up the stairs, forcing himself to slow down when he got to his bedroom. In his gray T-shirt and sweatpants, Louis was climbing into the top bunk.

Romeo kicked off his shoes and collapsed on the bottom bunk with an angry thump. Louis let out a loud yawn, and Ro heard him pull up the covers. Louis threw some stuff off his bed, including a Frisbee and a pair of jeans.

"Tired?" asked Romeo. He waited to see if Lou mentioned his phone call.

"Yeah," said Louis, oblivious to Ro's tone. "Night, bro. Night, Gary." Lou glanced at the mound on Gary's bed. "*He's* out like a light," he observed about Gary, sinking back into his pillow.

Romeo could barely contain himself. He stood up so he could see Louis. "So what were you and Peyton talking about for so long?" he sputtered.

"Hmmm?" mumbled Louis, without opening his mouth.

"Earlier, on the phone," said Romeo, tapping his hand on the bed. "You and Peyton." He stuffed a foam rubber ball into the toy basketball hoop on the side of the bed.

Louis thought a moment. "Oh, that was just about fencing and stuff," he said, turning away from Romeo. Shutting off the reading lamp near his bed, he settled under the covers. Lou pulled up the bright blue sheets and patchwork quilt.

Romeo pulled off his sweatbands with an angry snap. "Riiiiiight," he said. "Fencing." Wadding up the sweatbands, Romeo tried to toss them into the hamper and missed. Annoyed, he went over and stuffed them into the basket.

Louis rearranged the sheets again. "Yeah," Lou said. "We're going to be fencing partners." He reached under the covers and tossed a comic book on the floor.

Pulling pajamas out of his drawer, Romeo began to ramble. "Partners, right. Like people that stick together. Look out for each other. Loyal," he reflected. "Like you wouldn't, for example, keep a secret from your partner." Romeo moved closer to Louis, resting his elbows on the top bunk.

"No, you wouldn't," Romeo continued, not waiting for an answer. "And the more I think about it, having a partner is a lot like having a brother. You know what I mean?" He waited for Lou's response, but there was only silence.

Maybe what I said is sinking in, thought Ro. His

brother's silence told him he'd struck a chord, and Lou was absorbing what he'd said. Now Ro could launch into how angry he was about him and Peyton.

A couple seconds later, there was a loud snore. Ro shook his head, disgusted.

CHAPTER 6

GARY'S REVENGE

Jodi looked in the rearview mirror one more time. She and Ralston stumbled through a halting conversation, talking like strangers. The vibe between them had totally changed. She felt terrible.

At least it was almost over. After Gary showed up, the evening had taken a nosedive. How could she act normal with her baby brother sitting in the backseat?

Poor Ralston! He was clearly puzzled by her behavior. When he'd returned to the car after getting napkins, she was nervous and distant. Anxious to end the evening, she'd suggesting leaving the drive-in early.

Now they were parked in front of Ralston's house, and Jodi was waiting for him to leave.

"Nice night," Ralston ventured.

"Yeah," Jodi murmured, unable to think of anything more to say.

"So, thanks again for driving," he said. Jodi shrugged nervously.

"Hey, no biggie. Break, gas pedal, a little steering." Her giggle felt strained.

"Indeed," said Ralston, forcing a laugh.

Jodi spotted Gary in the rearview mirror again. Good grief! Ralston reached out to hold Jodi's hand but she blocked him with her other arm, pointing out the window. "Look, Roma Wilson walking her dog!" she exclaimed, hoping to distract him.

Ralston looked confused. "Jodi, Roma Wilson moved to Tacoma last year." Jodi fell silent. "Look, is there something going on here that I don't know about?" asked Ralston.

Gary smiled and waved from the back. "You might say that," Jodi said unhappily, trying to keep Ralston's attention on the front seat. She felt like she might burst into tears.

"Well, let's talk about it," said Ralston.

Jodi shook her head. The situation was beyond repair.

"Is it one of those embarrassing teenage inse-
curity issues?" asked Ralston. "Because I'm willing to
bare my soul."

Jodi cut him off. "Ralston, I'm tired. I'm sorry.
I have to go." She couldn't take another minute of
listening to him, knowing Gary was laughing in the
backseat. This date had gone on long enough.

"Oh. Okay," said Ralston, obviously hurt. "I'll
see you around." Without looking at her, he got out of
the car and shut the door. Jodi watched him walk to
his house, his back slumped. She looked at the leather
ceiling in despair.

Gary popped up in the backseat. "Aw, man . . . I
really wanted to hear him bare his soul," he said,
leaning on the armrest between the seats.

Jodi ignored him, trying to concentrate on getting home safely. Gary chattered on about Ralston, his
hair, his clothes, and aftershave until she wanted to
scream.

This night had been a disaster. Seeing Ralston
in school tomorrow would be totally embarrassing.
What could she say — that her brother had been in
the car with them the whole time? Ralston would feel

even more foolish. She thought about seeing Gary's face in the rearview mirror. . . . ugh!

Finally the Miller house came into view. Jodi pulled into the driveway, then threw the car keys at Gary before running into the house. She didn't stop running until she reached her bedroom and threw herself on her bed. She didn't even stop to visit with Angeline. She didn't want to talk to anyone.

All she wanted to do was hide.

Back in the car, Gary fingered the dinosaur key chain. He'd finally gotten his revenge on Jodi, but the moment felt different from the way he'd imagined it. Maybe he'd been too hard on Ralston.

But the guy had been pretty lame, saying "indeed" all the time. That aftershave was ridiculous. *And baring his soul?* thought Gary. *Give me a break!*

Still, he'd ruined her night. He remembered how excited she was talking on the phone to Ralston, and how she borrowed the red-and-silver necklace from Angeline. She had really, really liked him.

Gary remembered how she kept saying, "Doesn't he have the cutest name?"

After such an awkward date, Ralston and Jodi probably wouldn't go out again. And Ralston would never know why the date was so awful. Oh, well. At least she wouldn't be borrowing the car anytime soon.

Gary sank lower in the seat. His sister had broken his rules and used the car without his permission. She needed to be taught a lesson.

So why did he have a knot in the pit of his stomach?

The next morning, the breakfast table was a mess. A box of cereal had spilled over, and specks of orange juice dotted the red-and-white checked tablecloth. The first meal of the day was a rough-and-tumble affair at the Miller house. The breakfast table bore traces of the different foods everyone had eaten earlier: Jodi's granola, Angeline's fruit and yogurt, his dad's sweet roll, Gary's oatmeal. Romeo sat slumped in his chair, munching cornflakes like a zombie. He hadn't slept last night, thinking about Louis and Peyton. Romeo kept imagining what he'd say to Louis when he confronted him. So far this morning, they hadn't spoken.

But this morning, things were different.

He started to clear off the table, organizing a pile of books and papers. Angeline moved around the room, trying to clean up.

"Is this yours?" she asked Romeo, holding out a notebook.

Romeo barely looked up. "No, it's Louis's," he said, staring at the back of the cereal box. Angeline slipped some papers into the notebook, and Louis strolled in. He was wearing a new blue-and-white striped long-sleeved shirt, with the tags still attached.

"Well, look who's stylin' today," said Romeo, looking at the brand-new shirt, still creased from the package. Louis looked sheepish. "It's been sitting in the closet since Christmas," he explained.

Angeline offered to cut off the tags for him. Romeo persisted in his questioning. "So, months later, you just decided to bust it out for no reason?" he said angrily. He acted like a lawyer, making a case to a jury.

Louis shot him an uncertain look. "Uhhh, pretty much," he said. Angeline looked at Romeo sharply. "What's going on, Ro?" she asked, putting down the pair of scissors.

"I just think the whole situation is funny," said Romeo. "And I do know what's going on here!! I do!!!" He broke into a paranoid laugh. Angie raised her eyebrows, and she and Louis traded glances. What was up with him today?

Louis backed away from Ro and spoke with exaggerated slowness. "Okay, listen, I gotta go catch a spaceship back to *Earth*," he said, pointing outside. "I'll see ya later. . . ." He gave a wave and shut the door.

Romeo followed Lou to the door and opened it. "I hope they like the shirt!" he shouted after him. "On *Earth*," he added, slamming the door shut. Angeline looked at him carefully. "Seriously, what's going on?" she asked.

Ro crossed his arms. "He's going after my girl, Peyton," he said indignantly. "He knows I like her."

Angeline gave him a skeptical look as she cleared the breakfast table. "Alright, come on now," she said, carrying bowls to the sink.

Romeo grew more and more agitated. "Hello, the *shirt*," he said. "The two-hour phone call," he added, cradling his hand to look like a phone receiver. "It's obvious."

"Look, does Louis *know* that you like her?" asked Angeline, lowering her voice.

"Of course," said Romeo, dismissing her with his hand.

"Did you tell him?" asked Angeline.

"No," Ro admitted. "But I left a lotta hints. Hint here, hint there, pretty soon there were hints all over the place!" Romeo had talked about Peyton a lot, and Louis knew he sometimes walked her home from school. It was pretty obvious.

Angeline shook her head and smiled, putting her arm around Ro. "Listen, your brother would never sell you out," said Angeline. "You of all people should know that."

Romeo wasn't so sure. "Girls can make anyone act crazy," he argued.

Angeline looked at Ro meaningfully. "Uh-huh, and you just proved your point very nicely," she said. Ro looked at Angeline, surprised. *She means* me, he realized.

"I guess I did kinda lose it," he admitted, embarrassed. Maybe he *had* jumped the gun. His imagination

could get carried away sometimes. He blushed, thinking about scenes he'd conjured up: Lou and Peyton
going to the malt shop, movies, etc.

Angeline patted his shoulder. "Now get your
things, go to school and quit worrying," she said,
gathering her blueprints and ruler. Ro saw she was
ready to start work. Distractedly, he stuffed a notebook into his backpack.

He sure hoped she was right.

CHAPTER 7

FIGHTING WORDS

As Jodi raced out of the house, she heard a car honk outside. Gary was in the front seat of his car, reading a book. When he saw her coming, he closed his book and opened the door for her. "Hop in," he said.

Jodi sank into the passenger seat, wondering what Gary was up to. She had a drama club meeting in twenty minutes. "Listen, I've been doing some thinking," said Gary. "Thinking about my life, my family, where I'll be in twenty years."

He squinted, stroking his chin.

His sister shifted in her seat, impatient. Was this going to be another lecture from Gary on the care and feeding of his precious car? She was sorry she'd broken the rules, but hadn't she apologized?

She held her hand up to stop him. "Wrap it up, will ya?" she said. Gary handed her what appeared to be a stuffed parrot. Turning it over, she saw that it was attached to a silver key. "What's this?" she asked.

"It's a car key," said Gary. "For my car. I want you to have your own."

Jodi was stunned. "You do?" she asked, her heart pounding. Then her eyes narrowed. "Why are you doing this?" she asked.

"'Cuz I ruined your date," explained Gary. "And I want to make it up to you."

Jodi looked down at the strange stuffed animal in her hand. Her own car key! Was he serious? "Gary, that's very . . . mature of you," she said, not quite believing it. She squeezed the bird's feathers.

Gary shrugged. "Indeed," he said, imitating Ralston. Jodi gave him a look. "From now on, this'll be *our* car," said Gary.

"Really?" she squealed, fingering the dashboard. Gary thought for a moment.

"No," he said. "Not really. But from now on I'll be cooler about letting you use it. I promise."

Jodi was thrilled. Having use of the car would be awesome! She could go to the mall, or out for a movie. Her friends could organize a trip to a Sonics game or Fisherman's Wharf. She and Ralston could try again, she thought with a twinge. Maybe the art museum?

As Gary caressed the steering wheel, Jodi threw her arms around him. "Thank you, gimme a hug!" she cried, leaping to the driver's seat. Flooded with gratitude, Jodi wanted her brother to know how she felt.

Gary shrieked, burying his head in his chest to block her embrace. "Nooooooo!" he cried, running out of the car. He tried to wipe off the smell of her fruity perfume on his soccer jersey. Opening the screen door, he fled to safety.

He would share a car with his sister, but he wasn't going to let her hug him. *No way.*

Later, in class, the school bell jolted Romeo out of his daydream. His teacher, Mr. Frink, gave instructions in his usual weary monotone. "Before you leave," he said, "please put your homework papers on my desk so I can ruin my evening grading them." He waited for a laugh, but none came. He cleared his throat.

Romeo opened his notebook to find his homework. Inside was a piece of paper with Louis's handwriting on it. "Ode to a Thing of Beauty by Louis Testaverde," he read. What in the world . . . ?

He continued reading: "'It gives me chills when your wet nose tickles my earlobe.'"

He pushed the paper away in disgust. "That little girlfriend stealer!" he muttered to himself. Louis had obviously written this about Peyton. It was bad enough knowing Louis liked her. Now he had to read his love poems?

Looking up, he saw someone in full fencing gear walking by the door. Ro looked at the mesh mask and white vest. It had to be his brother.

"Yo, Louis!" he shouted. He shut the notebook and grabbed his backpack. Mr. Frink looked at him. "Romeo? Your homework?"

Tossing the notebook onto his teacher's desk, Romeo tore out of the room with the poem in his hand.

"It's in there somewhere," he shouted to a confused Mr. Frink. The teacher looked at the mess on his desk and sighed.

Romeo stormed into the cafeteria. There he was! Mr. Three Musketeers wannabe all alone, practicing his thrusts and parries. He had to admit Louis had gotten pretty good. For a moment, he just stood there, watching.

"Hey, yo, big shot!" Romeo yelled, shaking himself back to life and waving the ode. "Why are you trying to steal my girl?" The fencer turned toward him. "Don't act like you don't know what I'm talking about," he roared. "I'm talking about Peyton."

Louis began leaping and slashing his sword in a series of lightning-swift moves. "Would you cool it with the sword?" Romeo demanded. "You don't even know how mad I am right now. All these years we've shared a room . . . every secret," he said.

Romeo kept going, not waiting for a response. "We've even shared underwear," he bellowed. "Though not on purpose," he added.

Louis brandished the sword again, showing off his dazzling fighting skills. He held his sword at Ro's chest. "You wanna do that to your bro — I said, will you cool it with that thing?" Ro repeated, exasperated.

His opponent playfully poked at Ro again, piercing his orange football jersey. Ro retreated until he was backed against the cafeteria wall with a huge McDaniel Knights logo painted on it. His back grazed the cinderblock wall.

Apparently, Louis would rather fight than talk. Well, Romeo could do that, too.

"Alright," Ro threatened. "I'm gonna get all pirate on you." He began to pantomime a fighting maniac. Grabbing a sword off the table, he went into a mad samurai dance, swinging wildly and whooping like a crazed warrior.

He tore off his wristband and slanted it on his head like a pirate patch. He ran headlong into Lou, swinging the foil and shrieking, "Yaaaaaaaaaaaaaaaaa hhhhhh!"

Louis easily knocked the sword out of Ro's hand and picked it up, waving both weapons. Then he plucked at Ro some more, and flipped the sword back to Ro with his foot. Ro caught it with one hand. "Oh, it's like that, huh?" Ro said.

Ro tore off the wristband and picked up a fenc-ing mask. He pulled it over his face, not even bothering to fasten the strap. "I didn't want to do this to my own brother, but . . ." he declared. "It's on!"

Now the two fighters went at it full force. On one side of the lunch counter, Ro took a swipe at Louis, and a tower of plastic cups went flying. A spray of metal forks and spoons followed, starting an ava-lanche of green trays.

Ro ran for cover behind the serving counter. With a samurai grunt, he slashed a box, and a cascade of hair nets came tumbling down. They landed on the two fighters like snowflakes. Romeo's opponent shook them off and dived at him over the counter.

Desperate, Ro grabbed a handful of ketchup packets and pelted them at his brother. No rules in love and war, right?

Putting down his sword, he grabbed a broom, swinging it like a foil. Leaving the shelter of the coun-ter, he parried with his new weapon. But the long brush made him stumble. He threw the broom at Lou and picked up the sword again.

Like a wild man, Ro jumped on a metal cart for stacking trays, using it as a shield while Louis stabbed at him through the slots.

Then Louis jumped on the cart, too, and the two figures spun around the cafeteria, ricocheting off the walls like bumper cars. Just as he was about to crash, Romeo took a dive onto one of the tables, and his sword went skidding across the floor.

Louis leaped and cornered Romeo, knocking him backward over the table, flipping him onto the floor. Finally, Ro's opponent had him pinned to the ground, sword to his chest. Romeo held up his hands in surrender.

Just then, the cafeteria door opened. Romeo looked up and saw a fencing student walk in . . . it was Louis.

Huh?

"Ro?" said Louis, shocked to see him splayed out on the ground. Why was Romeo in a fencing mask? Who was his partner?

"Louis?!" Ro sputtered in disbelief. If that was his brother, who had he been fighting all this time?

He looked up. The fencer pulled off the mask. A mass of black corkscrew curls fell out of the wire mesh. A hair ornament appeared, along with a familiar set of flashing brown eyes. He couldn't believe what he saw.

All along, his opponent had been Peyton.

CHAPTER 8

UNMASKED

Romeo fell back on the floor, now utterly defeated. He couldn't believe he'd been fighting Peyton all this time, thinking it was Louis. He shut his eyes. What had he said to her?

He felt ridiculous. Why hadn't he checked to make sure it was Louis under the mask? When he saw the fencing outfit, he'd just assumed it was his brother. It never occurred to him it could be someone else — much less Peyton!

Instead, he had raved like a maniac to the very person he was trying to win over. He had bullied, threatened, and made a lot of wild accusations. She'd seen him at his very worst. She probably couldn't stand him now.

"Uhhhhhhhhhhhhh," he groaned. Peyton shook out her hair and looked at the two brothers. She said to Ro, "I think you two need to talk." She tucked her mask and sword under her arm and left them alone in the lunchroom. Romeo watched the door swing shut.

Nice going, thought Romeo. *Always a good idea to engage in physical combat with the girl you have a crush on, then frighten her with a jealous rant.* No wonder she had cleared out so fast. She was probably reporting him to the principal.

Louis was totally confused. "What happened, bro?" asked Louis. Why had Romeo and Peyton been dueling? And why had his brother looked so surprised when Peyton pulled off her mask?

Come to think of it, Romeo had been acting strange for a couple of days. Ever since Louis had joined the fencing team, in fact. First, Louis had found him hanging around after school to "clean his locker." Then Ro seemed obsessed with fencing, asking lots of questions about the club.

Plus, there were other things. Romeo had bad-gered him endlessly about his phone call last night, and had seemed disgruntled this morning. He'd practically jumped down Louis's throat about wearing a new shirt to school. Now Romeo was standing in the middle of a sea of silverware, paper, and plastic. The place was trashed.

"It looks like World War Two in here," observed Louis, looking around.

Romeo turned around, taking in the mess that surrounded him. He had to deal with this disaster before Mr. Frink or Principal Ramawad saw it. "I gotta clean this up," he said.

"I'm on it," said Louis, picking up plates and cups.

Romeo looked at his brother warily, not sure if he should accept his help. He was still mad at him about Peyton. How could Louis explain the phone call, the secrets, and the poem?

As if reading his mind, Louis said, "C'mon, let's just get this out of the way first. Then you can tell me why you've been acting psycho."

"Me?" protested Romeo, dropping a stack of cups. "You're the one who . . ." he began. Just then they heard voices in the hall. Principal Ramawad! Ro looked around frantically.

"Help me with these ketchup packs, will you?" Ro said instead. Their confrontation would have to wait.

Louis surveyed the damage, spotting slash marks on his brother's pants.

"Wow," he said, impressed. "She really whipped your butt."

Half an hour later, the two brothers sat in the hallway, bouncing a basketball against a wall of lockers. Romeo wore his gray sweatshirt with the hood up, as if he wanted to hide his face.

"So then, when I found your poem, I just guessed it was about Peyton," Ro confessed to Louis.

Louis caught the basketball. "Man, you know I wouldn't do that to you." He laughed to himself, thinking about Mrs. Guthrie's golden retriever. Talk about being off base!

Romeo wasn't convinced. "But what about last night on the phone, when she was all 'don't tell Romeo'?" Ro imitated in a squeaky voice. "And you're all 'he won't hear it from me'?" Romeo felt himself getting worked up all over again.

"Dude," said Louis in disbelief. "You listened to my phone call?"

Ro nodded, ashamed to admit it. Louis shook his head, exasperated. Ro was really over the edge. What was next, putting a tape recorder in his locker? Did Romeo have so little trust in him? Hearing about Ro spying on him made him angry.

"You don't have to tell me if you don't want," said Romeo, with a sigh. Listening in on someone's phone call was uncool. He remembered telling Angeline that girls could make anyone crazy, and Angeline telling Ro he'd proved his own point.

A metal door clanged shut, and both boys noticed Peyton at her locker at the other end of the hall. From a distance, they saw she was no longer in fencing gear. In a white ruffled skirt and banana scoop-necked blouse, Peyton made a completely different impression.

No one would guess she was the fierce fighter who'd demolished Ro only an hour ago. She continued putting her books away, apparently unaware that they were watching her.

Louis looked at Ro's sad face. It was time to get serious. "Ro, Peyton likes you."

"She does?" said Ro, uncertainly.

"Yeah," said Louis. "A lot. Like, an-hour-and-a-half-on-the-phone a lot. She just wanted to find out if you were a player." He rolled the ball back to Romeo.

Romeo took the ball and spun it on his fingertips. "What'd you say?"

Louis shrugged. "I told her the truth," he said. Romeo's mouth dropped open, and his eyes widened. *Uh-oh*, he thought.

"That you're the coolest guy I know," said Louis, very matter-of-factly.

Romeo felt weak with relief. He smiled and bounced the ball on his knee. "That's my boy," he said, punching Louis on the shoulder.

For a moment, Romeo shut his eyes in gratitude. Why had he ever doubted Louis? His brother had always stuck up for him. Maybe things were okay, after all.

Suddenly Peyton was standing over them, smiling shyly. Ro noticed how her hair ornament matched her shirt. She put down her white backpack and looked from one of them to the other.

"So, are you two friends again?" she asked.

Lou looked at Ro. "I think we're good," he said.

"Real good," Ro added.

"Good," said Peyton. She and Romeo smiled at each other. Louis noticed them and took his cue. "Ya know what," Lou said, standing up and backing away, "I'd better go change. Be right back." Before they could respond, he was gone.

Sprinting down the hall, Louis thought about Romeo. How could he not know Peyton was crazy about him? She had a mad crush on the guy. Maybe they'd finally get together.

"Bye, Louis," said Peyton, not taking her eyes off Ro as he got up to stand beside her. But Louis had already disappeared. Ro smiled back.

"I gotta run," she said, zipping up her jacket. She smiled and turned toward the staircase, hoisting up her white backpack. A bunch of key chains dangled from it: a blue rabbit's foot, a tiny soccer ball, and a cowboy boot.

Romeo called after her. "Hey, Peyton, tell me

something," he begged. "How come you didn't tell me it was you behind the mask?" he asked. His voice echoed down the hall.

Peyton stopped on the stairs and answered with her back turned away from Ro. She shut her eyes for a moment. "'Cuz, I was hoping I might find out who the Mystery Girl was." She turned around, and their eyes met. "And I did," she said, smiling.

Romeo was happy. Peyton knew he liked her, and she liked him back. He and Louis were tighter than ever. He'd acted silly, but somehow it had all turned out okay. Better than okay.

Ro smiled broadly, and Peyton waved a backward good-bye. Alone in the hall, he did his own little happy dance, skipping, clapping, and jumping wildly in the air. After a spin, and a moonwalk, he pantomimed a perfect jump shot.

CHAPTER 9

THE RAP-OFF

Romeo stood in an alley in downtown Seattle, listening to a rapper entertaining the crowd. *Not bad,* he thought to himself, nodding his head to the beat. It was his first time at a rap-off, and he was up next.

He had watched each competitor take a turn, bragging about why he deserved to be the winner. Against a fence plastered with posters and graffiti, a group of about thirty kids stood cheering and clapping. The asphalt was wet with last night's rain.

Nodding his head to the beat, Romeo felt his palms get wet. This guy was good! This afternoon was a free-for-all, where anyone could take a turn. Today's winner would continue the battle at Club Limit, and get a crack at taking down the reigning champ.

The featured rapper was big and bald, with a gray knit cap and a gold hoop earring. With broad hand gestures and a swaggering style, he sang out his rhyme:

> *"Check it, my rhymes shine like a*
> *Diamond in a necklace*
> *So sick, I spray the mike*
> *With disinfectant. . . ."*

You're as good as he is, Romeo tried to persuade himself. He knew he had the moves, the cool, the attitude . . . so why was he suddenly so nervous? Entering the competition had seemed like a good idea, but now he dreaded it.

As the rapper kept pounding out his rhyme, Romeo became increasingly nervous. He was used to being backed up by his band and playing to friendly audiences. This group looked older and harder to please. Each new contestant had to prove himself.

It didn't help that he was younger — and smaller — than everyone else. At fourteen, he had to be one of the youngest rappers at the club. It was hard to brag about how tough you were against guys who had been out in the real world, not just the halls of McDaniel High School.

The bald rapper continued his rant:

"Effortless drop sentences to records
Got the freshness from the entrance till I exit
Now you know I'm hot like the Equator at the limit
You have to bring it to your ears with no fear
If not, then your career's finished."

After he finished, people cheered and slapped him on the back. Romeo waited for the applause to die down. Next to Mr. Big and Bald, he felt like a pipsqueak. The crowd grew silent again, as Romeo stepped up to the mike.

The audience seemed taken aback by his size. In his baggy gray tank and white wristbands, Romeo looked young. Ro saw people exchange glances. Who was this kid? A guy in a leather vest looked at him skeptically. A woman with spiky hair rolled her eyes.

The bald rapper seemed relieved to see how young his competitor was. He smiled and stepped back, as if to say, "Beating this kid won't be as hard I thought."

People folded their arms, waiting. *This isn't going to be easy*, thought Romeo. He took a deep breath, and dove in.

> *"Look, you know who it is*
> *No other than the kid*
> *Cool as the ice*
> *That I wear on my wrist*
> *Call me L'il Ro or Billy the Kid*
> *Y'all does it small,*
> *We does it big —"*

Hearing murmurs of approval, Ro's voice grew louder and more confident. He felt loose and playful, making eye contact and hand gestures. Strutting around proudly, he unleashed his sassiest rhymes.

> *"You know how I get down*
> *On the billboard charts*
> *At the top where I'm found*

Recognized all over town
'Cuz I make hot raps using verbs and nouns."

The crowd screamed and clapped. *They like me,* Romeo thought, hugely relieved. He took off his base-ball cap, and put it on again. The audience clapped furiously.

Out of the crowd stepped Loshe, the owner of Club Limit, and emcee of the rap battle. With his unshaven face and streaked 'fro, Loshe looked like an eccentric hipster-artist. His diamond ear stud glinted as he took the mike and spoke in a silky announcer's voice.

"A lot of talent here," he said, looking over the crowd. "*A lot* of talent. It's hard to choose," he said, letting the tension build. "Anyone else want to step up?" he asked.

No one came forward. "Alright," said Loshe. As the contest judge, he based his decision on audience response. The crowd leaned forward, and some peo-ple called out their favorites.

Loshe turned to Romeo, who was fiddling with

his dog tags. "Youngster, you won the battle today," he declared.

The crowd roared, and people rushed to give Ro high fives. Giddy with excitement, Ro went to high-five Loshe, but the club owner withdrew his hand. "Hey, man," said Ro, holding out his palm. "A little help?"

Loshe gave him a tight smile. "You're gonna need it against Lo Key." He started to hand out flyers, and Romeo grabbed one. In graffiti-style lettering, the flyer read: CLUB LIMIT RAP-OFF THIS WEEKEND, FEATURING LO KEY.

"If he lives up to his hype, I will," said Romeo. Next to him was a young, red-headed girl in a black denim jacket and green scarf. She looked over at him and smiled.

"I heard Lo Key brought it on so strong, that cat made Busta cry. . . ." said Loshe, his eyes taunting Romeo.

"And Ludakris leave town," added the bald guy in the knit cap. Other people chimed in with their own stories about Lo Key.

Before Ro could respond, his cell phone rang.

He picked it up, straining to hear it above the noisy crowd. "Hello?" he said, cupping his ear.

Jodi's voice cut him off. "Yeah, hello," she said angrily. "It's six o'clock and we're at rehearsal. Where are you?"

Romeo scanned the chaotic scene around him. "I'm at the . . . uh . . . library," he said. "Sit tight, I'll be right there." He clicked off the phone, turning to Loshe.

"See you at the battle," he shouted, running off down the alley. He wove through the crowd, waving the flyer in the air. "I'm in the rap-off!" he sang to himself. "Yeah, I made it!"

There was only one problem. What was he going to tell his family? So far, he had kept the rap-off a secret. That way if he failed, no one would know about it, he had reasoned.

Today's battle would have been ten times harder if Jodi, Lou, or anyone in his family had been there. He thought about the tough crowd, waiting for him to prove himself. If he'd tanked, he'd have been totally humiliated. No, it was safer not to tell anyone.

It felt strange to lie, but it was only for a few days — until the final battle was over. It wasn't such a big deal, he told himself. He looked at the flyer and stuffed it in his pocket. He'd share the good news with them after he'd won.

Skipping down the street, he punched the air with his fist.

By six-thirty, Romeo still hadn't shown up at rehearsal. Lou, Gary, and Jodi sat around the garage, bored. Without Romeo, they couldn't get much done. Lou turned to Jodi suddenly. "Why don't you just do the rap?" he asked.

Jodi sighed. "I can't do the rap," she said. "I do the beats. Romeo does the raps." Their band, the Romeo Show, had always featured Romeo as the lead vocalist. Why change it now?

"Whatever," said Louis, stepping up to the mike. In a deep announcer's voice, he said, "Now pinch-hitting for Romeo is . . . Mad Lou." He took a bow and turned to Gary. "Can you give me a beat?"

Gary shrugged, and flicked some buttons on the console, and Lou grabbed the mike. With stiff, jerky motions, he tried to imitate Romeo's fluid rap style. But his words came out clumsy and halting:

"I'm Mad Lou
That's mad Lou to you
I'm a mad rapper
How do you do?"

As he sang his rhymes, he made rigid arm movements, as if directing traffic. His exaggerated gestures were the opposite of Romeo's smooth, subtle moves. Strutting around the room, he knocked a paper lantern off the ceiling, waving his arm above his head.

He stopped and smiled. Jodi and Gary stared in disbelief, and then looked at each other. Was he serious?

Louis looked at his siblings. "C'mon, I'm not that bad," he insisted. They looked at him again. "Am I?" he squeaked. In unison, Gary and Jodi nodded yes.

Lou started to argue with them. "But wait, you haven't even heard my best stuff. . . ." he said.

Just then Romeo flew in the door. He wiped the sweat off his face and removed his wristbands. Taking a long swig from his water bottle, he sank into an armchair. Everyone looked at him.

"About time," said Jodi sharply.

"Oh, sorry, guys," Romeo apologized. "Don't hate. I was studying."

They all looked at him skeptically. "Yeah, right," said Gary, snorting.

"What?" said Romeo. "I have a big biology test on Friday." The group traded glances. "Whatever," said Jodi wearily. "Let's take it from the top."

Louis started them off. "Five, six, seven, eight . . ."

Romeo got up and took the mike. "Head, shoulders, knees, toes/Party over here/Take it to the flow. . . ." he belted. He tackled his rhymes with a new energy as the music washed over him.

Jodi felt her body relax into the delicious groove. The group blended seamlessly, creating lush sounds and a funky rhythm. Even when they fought, music always brought them together. She and Louis smiled at each other.

Jodi closed her eyes, hoping nothing ever came between them.

*   *   *

The next morning, Louis carried an all-terrain board and orange helmet down a steep hill. Gary trailed behind, lugging a video camera and a police radar to record speed. Louis had bought a used radar at a garage sale — no one had realized what he had planned.

Louis and Gary were on the outskirts of town, near a parking lot filled with old school buses. The Seattle skyline stretched behind them. In the morning sun, the Space Needle glittered over the city.

"We have to get to school," Gary reminded him.

Louis put the skateboard down. "This is more important than school, Gary," he explained. "This is about my legacy. I'm about to break the downhill ATB speed record for a kid under sixteen," he announced. "And you're my witness."

"But the record is fifty-seven miles per hour," Gary pointed out.

"Then all I gotta do is go fifty-eight," said Lou.

Gary looked doubtful. "Let's say a car comes," he said.

"No cars are gonna come," Lou said, pointing to a sign: ROAD CLOSED BY CITY ORDINANCE. There were blockades at each end of the street. The road had been blocked off for months.

Even without cars, Gary was dubious. This seemed like one of Louis's more unlikely schemes. Why did his brother think he could beat records set by serious athletes? Whenever Gary had seen him shred, Lou had ended up on his butt.

Still, Gary had agreed to help him. If Lou really did grab some sick air, Gary wanted to see it with his own eyes. And if he wiped out, Gary didn't want to miss that, either.

At the top of the hill, Louis looked down at the steep route ahead of him. He strapped on his helmet and knee pads, getting into position. "Alright," he said. "Let's do this." Lou asked Gary if everything was ready, and Gary nodded.

"Camera?" asked Lou.

"Check," he said. The tripod was parked mid-point on the hill.

"Speed radar?" asked Louis.

Gary held up the black box. "Check."

Louis tightened his knee pads. "The next time you see me, I'll have made history," he said. "Go on."

Gary ran down to the middle of the hill and readied the camera as Lou put on his padding. Lou looked ahead. "It's go time," he said, flipping his helmet down. Gary looked through the video camera and gave him a thumbs-up.

Louis mounted the board and took off flying down the hill. "I'm doing it!" he yelled. Gary looked up from the camera and saw Lou heading straight for him. "Gary, get out of the way!" Louis yelled.

Gary panicked. Louis was hurtling straight toward him! He screamed and dived into the bushes, dropping the radar. Louis swerved to avoid tripping over it, hitting a bump instead. "Whoooooaaaah!" he yelled. He sailed into the air and landed in a pile of garbage.

Afraid to look, Gary covered his face. After a moment of silence, he removed his hands. "That had to hurt," he said, running toward Louis, who was buried under a pile of green trash bags. Gary began to dig him out, tossing bags away.

"Louis, are you alright?" he asked, pulling bags out.

"Mmmm-hmmm," murmured Louis.

Gary checked the radar. "Well, you only went thirty-one miles per hour," he said. "But maybe you broke the record for the most air?" With that, Gary dissolved into giggles. Sometimes he cracked himself up.

Louis took off his helmet and spit out some food. "Gross!" cried Gary. Looking down at the chicken chow mein he'd just spit out, Louis fell back into the garbage. Gary laughed and threw a bag on top of him.

Lou sighed. It was going to be a long morning.

CHAPTER 10

THE BIG LIE

Later that afternoon, Romeo sat on the floor in the school hallway. Bent over his rhyme book, he tried out a few lines. "I've got the flow to drop," he wrote. Frowning, he crossed it out. "I've got the flow to stop," he tried again. That wasn't right, either.

Someone snatched the book out of his hand. Ro looked up and saw his friend Myra, grinning. "Hello, Romeo," she said in a teasing voice. Her eyes sparkled behind rectangular red glasses. With her long, curly blond hair and colorful frames, she had her own funky style.

"Myra, are you crazy?" he asked, grabbling the book back. "Don't be messing with a man who's laying down his rhymes." Myra and he had become good buddies in the last year, but she still drove him nuts. He looked up and saw she was with a friend.

"Sorry, I'm just messing with you," said Myra, pushing back her glasses. "But I do have someone who wants to meet you. Romeo, this is my cousin, Melissa."

Romeo looked at the red-headed girl next to Myra. She was dressed in peach silk and black denim. There was something familiar about her. "Hey, Melissa," he nodded hello. "You just transfer to McDaniel?" he asked.

Melissa lifted her chin up. "No, I go to South Highland," she explained. "But our school's closed today for asbestos inspection." Her manner was polite but distant.

"Don't I know you, though?" Romeo asked. Had he seen her in the neighborhood, or at the mall?

"I don't know, do you?" Melissa answered back in a teasing voice.

"You work at the Freezy Cone?" he guessed.

Melissa laughed. "Nice try. I was at the rap-off yesterday," she said. *Bingo*, thought Romeo. "I saw you battle," said Melissa, looking him over. "You're pretty good."

Romeo shrugged off her praise. "Thanks," he said, smiling. "I was in the zone. It takes a crazy amount of focus and concentration to really get in the flow," he explained.

"Oh, I see," said Melissa.

Myra broke into a smile. "We can't wait," she said, referring to the battle.

Romeo adjusted his black baseball cap. "Alright, so I'll see y'all later — and I promise to tear it up."

"Tear what up?" Louis asked, walking by.

Ro sprang to his feet. "The 'zine," said Ro, blurting out the first thing that popped into his head. "Your 'zine. I read it and I tear it up," said Romeo, grabbing Louis's arm to distract him.

Louis was confused. A few months ago he'd started his own 'zine, called "Lou's World," as an alternative to the school newspaper. To his surprise, it had been a big hit. "Wait," said Louis, trying to understand. "You tore my 'zine up?"

Ro grabbed Louis to steer him away from the girls. Keeping this secret was getting complicated. He guided Louis down the hall. "Hey, bro," he said. "Can't you tell when I'm kidding?"

Louis shrugged, not following. "If you say so," he said.

Later that day, Romeo practiced basketball in the school yard. He dribbled, spun around, and laid in a perfect finger roll. Spotting Myra's blue knit poncho, he walked over to her, still bouncing the ball. "Yo, Myra," he called.

"Hey, Romeo," she greeted him. "Walk me home?"

"Sure," said Romeo, trying a hook shot. "But I got a favor to ask."

Myra nodded, playing with the fringe on her poncho. She and Romeo hadn't always had the easiest friendship. Ever since they were kids, she'd had a crush on him. But they'd gotten to be good friends, and he often sought out her advice about school, family, and girls.

"The thing I'm doing tonight isn't really a band thing," he explained. "It's more of an individual challenge." He started to pass the ball to her, then faked her out and did a layup shot.

Myra smiled playfully. "Okay," she said. "Call a girl with a one hundred and sixty IQ dumb, but I still haven't heard what the favor is."

Romeo tried to explain. "You see, all the great rappers were great battlers," he began. "Jay-Z, Nas, Mos Def. I just want to see how good I am. One-on-one." His voice started to rise. "And I don't want Louis or anyone else knowing I'm going down there."

Myra looked up at him. "This Lo Key is supposed to be off the hook," she remarked. "What if you lose?"

Romeo tossed his basketball up and caught it behind his back. "If I lose, fair enough," he said. "I just want to see how good I am."

Myra looked amused. "But do you really need to keep it a secret from your family?" she asked.

Ro stopped dribbling for a moment. "Well, if they know I'm doing this, they'll probably worry," he reasoned. "And I figure, why go through all that drama?"

Myra assured him that they wouldn't hear anything from her. *Cool*, thought Romeo, dunking the ball into the net. So why was he still uneasy?

*   *   *

Romeo stared at the clock in the garage. It was 7:45 already. He could barely hide his impatience while Jodi chatted on and on.

"... Which is why I think we should make the verse the chorus, and the chorus the verse," she argued. "Know what I mean?" She looked at Romeo, expecting a response.

"Yeah, sure, whatever," he said. His mind was a thousand miles away, thinking about Lo Key. Was he one of those body-builder types, covered in tattoos? Or maybe he'd be dripping with diamonds, pulling up to the club in a white Rolls Royce. . . .

Jodi checked off a line on her list and continued. "Last thing," she said. "Hacksaw needs us to put together some material for an album." Hacksaw was their manager, a colorful character who really knew the music biz.

Romeo looked up. "He got us a record deal?" he asked excitedly. The group had dreamed for years of getting signed to a label.

"No," said Jodi. "But he wants us to be ready. Says when the time comes, it'll happen fast." She pulled a list of songs out of her black notebook. "He wants us to choose our ten favorites."

Ro took the list and handed it back to her without looking at it. "I like 'em all," he said. Jodi shoved the paper back in his face. "Okay, but which ones do you like most?" she asked, annoyed.

He looked at the clock again. "Do we really have to do this now?" he pleaded. "I have to get back to the library."

Jodi put the paper down and looked at him. "You're going to the library?" she asked, incredulously. "Again?"

Romeo looked down at his black and silver sneakers. "Remember, I got that history test," he reminded her.

Jodi folded her arms. "You said your test was in biology," she said, narrowing her eyes. Romeo had to think fast. "It's . . . uh . . . the history of biology," he said lamely. "And I gotta go." He grabbed his baseball cap and ran.

Jodi watched the door slam, suspicious. It didn't add up. If her brother was so studious all of a sudden, why wasn't he carrying any books?

CHAPTER 11

LEFT BEHIND

Louis stood in the boys' bedroom. On top of his head, he was balancing three bricks. Gary stood next to him, looking at his stopwatch. In his other hand, he held a video camera.

"How'm I doing?" asked Louis.

"Great," Gary said dryly. "You only have thirty-two seconds, twenty-four hours, and six days to go."

Louis was unfazed. No one ever said breaking a world record was easy. He tried to scratch his nose without toppling the bricks. Angeline passed by the room and saw Louis with a strange pile on his head.

"Is this something I should be concerned about?" she asked with mock seriousness.

Louis shifted his weight. Now his ear itched.

"Nope," he said. "Just planning my entry into celebrity." Angeline rolled her eyes.

Jodi passed by the room and did a double take. "What are you guys doing?" she asked, taking in the bricks and the video camera.

"I'm trying to find my 'thing,'" said Louis.

"What thing?" asked Jodi.

The bricks started to wobble dangerously. Louis adjusted his balance to avoid a collapse. "My thing," he explained. "You're a great student, Romeo is a great rapper, Gary is . . ."

"Brilliant, cute, financial wizard . . ." Gary finished for him.

". . . short," finished Louis. Gary threw a shoe at him.

Angeline interjected. "Louis, you started your own 'zine. You're in a band. I say you've got plenty of 'things' going on," she argued.

Louis looked at her, then up at the bricks. "Ang, a grand total of twenty people read my 'zine. Five of them live in this house. I need to leave my mark on history," he said dramatically. "You know . . . who is Louis Testaverde? What will people know him for?"

Jodi thought for a moment. "Referring to himself in the third person?" she suggested, with a smile.

Louis started to wobble again. Above him, the tower of bricks wavered dangerously. He dashed around the room, trying to keep the bricks from falling. "Uh-oh, no, no . . ." he stammered.

The bricks came flying down with a crash, flinging Louis into a shelving unit. The shelves tumbled, starting an avalanche of books, toys, and CDs. Gary held up his hands to avoid being pelted by a spray of plastic action figures.

Sprawled on the floor, Louis picked puzzle pieces, coins, and a sock out of his hair. "Arghhhh!" he cried. "That didn't work."

Gary laughed. "Don't worry," he said. "I've got it on tape." This was almost as good as Louis skateboarding into a mountain of garbage.

They all bent down to look at the monitor on Gary's video camera. He replayed the footage showing Louis's scream, followed by a blizzard of bricks and toys.

Jodi and Angeline giggled, but then felt guilty. Poor Lou! Ang went over to give him a hand. "You okay?" she asked.

He nodded as Angeline started sifting through the wreckage. She picked up a green plastic dinosaur, a baseball, and then a crumpled piece of paper. It was a flyer that read: RAP BATTLE AT CLUB LIMIT.

"A rap battle?" she asked the others.

Jodi took the flyer just as Angie's cell phone rang. Angeline moved out of the room, and the kids looked at the flyer carefully.

"The rap battle is tonight. . . ." said Jodi, her eyes flashing. "And Romeo just left." She shook her head. "He said he was going to the 'library.'"

Louis made the connection. "Are you thinking what I'm thinking?" he said.

Jodi nodded. "He didn't go to the library; he went to the rap battle."

Grabbing the flyer out of Jodi's hands, Lou examined it, stunned, "I can't believe he didn't tell us about this."

Jodi tried to puzzle it out. "Why wouldn't he. . . ."

she said. "Unless he's planning to leave the group . . . ?"
Louis crumpled up the flyer with this fist. The siblings
looked at each other fearfully.

They'd never had secrets from each other
before. Why would Romeo give a performance without
telling them? Had he been approached about doing a
solo act? He had always been the featured talent . . .
maybe he didn't need them anymore.

Lou thought about how Ro was always writing
in his rhyme book, pushing himself creatively. Did he
think the group was holding him back?

Gary recalled how fans sometimes mobbed the
band after concerts — maybe he wanted the attention
for himself.

Jodi wondered if having a family band was
beginning to seem childish to a hot young rapper.

Back in the garage, the kids paced back and
forth. "I am so mad right now," Jodi sputtered. "I
can't even think straight. How could Ro betray us like
this?" She picked up one of their demo CDs and
slammed it down in disgust.

Louis smoothed back his spiky hair. "Look, guys, let's not get all riled up," he said. "I've been working on my rap skills. Gary, give me a beat."

Jodi and Gary looked up. Was he joking? Lou was a terrible rapper. He recited rhymes like he was reading a math book.

Gary hit his forehead with his hand and laid down a track. Louis jumped on it, spewing words in a high-pitched whine. With jerky motions, he worked the stage, trying to imitate Ro's loose-limbed style. He spit out his words in an awkward jumble:

> *"I'm Mad Lou*
> *That's Mad Lou to you*
> *Back off and let me flow*
> *You interrupt, I'll blow. . . ."*

Jodi and Gary stared at him, and then looked at each other. "I'm gonna kill Romeo," said Jodi slowly, gritting her teeth. "Come on," she said to Gary. "I'm leaving."

Lou stopped in mid-rhyme. Okay, so maybe he

wasn't ready to be their front man yet. He just needed a little more practice. Putting the mike down, he ran off to join his brother and sister.

They had to find out what Ro was up to.

CHAPTER 12

THE BATTLE

Club Limit was packed. Romeo waited near the stage, taking in the wild scene. Hundreds of people waved their arms back and forth, moving to the music. The whole place was pulsating with energy.

In back of him was a giant banner that said CLUB LIMIT in copper graffiti letters. Romeo stood off to the side, decked out in a blue-and-yellow football jersey with matching wristbands. He pulled nervously at his dog tags.

His opponent was up first. Mister Z was a tall, fierce guy with a shaved head and knit cap, and wearing a long blue jacket over his sweatshirt. With sweeping arm gestures, he sang to Romeo, taunting him with put-downs:

"Yeah, I got a couple lines for the lil' kid Romeo
He already lost and he doesn't even know
Just go and hide your head in shame
For even thinking you could play me in this rap
   game."

He seemed to snarl his words, strutting around the stage with confidence. Oozing attitude, he looked outraged to be competing with a kid, especially one who barely came up to his chest. He treated Romeo like a fly he wanted to swat away.

The crowd responded with oohs and aahs. Romeo stepped up for his turn, sweating under the bright lights. He took a deep breath, then turned to the first rapper and let loose.

"You know who I am
You know what I'm about
Lil' Rome is the king of this Freestyle Platinum
What you hearing coming out my mouth
So many cars look like
A Dillard ship
In front my house

And I don't mean to brag
But I just bought the mall
I'm gonna need some bigger bags
Uh, I got the game from my dad
We roll like trucks on them twenty-six mags
You know I go hard once my flow start,
Too hot to cool off
You don't want to battle me
'Cuz I'm the greatest in the ring
Like Muhammed Ali."

The audience roared their approval. Romeo smiled, and the opponents touched fists briefly. Loshe, the club owner, took the mike.

"Player, player . . . wow!" he said, pointing at Romeo. "The youngster has some game." Romeo played with his wristbands.

To Mister Z, he said, "You need to sit down and get educated." The rapper shook his head and scowled. Loshe announced to the crowd, "Romeo moves up." He had won the round! Each round eliminated a contender, until the two best rappers were left to compete in the final battle.

The crowd applauded loudly. "Give it up for Romeo," Loshe yelled, opening his arms. Romeo adjusted his baseball cap, waved, and walked off with a swagger.

Stepping down from the stage, Romeo was hit with a flashing light. "Smile!" shouted Myra, looking sleek in a high-necked jacket and shimmering green skirt and holding a digital camera.

Next to Myra was her cousin, Melissa. "Hey, you made it," Ro greeted them warmly. In a silver belted jacket and widely ripped jeans, Melissa looked fantastic. In fact, he barely recognized her.

"We wouldn't miss this for the world," said Myra with a smile. "Let me get a picture of you two." Melissa slid next to Romeo and turned to him. She was wearing makeup, Ro noticed. Maybe that's why she looked so different, he thought.

"Caught you on stage," she said. "You rocked the mike."

Romeo nodded. "True that," he admitted.

Melissa looked at him challengingly, "You ready for Lo Key?" she asked.

Romeo shrugged. "Haven't seen him yet," he

said. "Maybe he heard a little of the Rome flow and decided to take the night off," he chuckled wishfully.

Melissa raised her eyebrow.

"Smile!" shouted Myra. As the flash went off, Ro and Melissa both grinned. Melissa turned to respond to Romeo.

"I don't think so," she said. "Whoever wins the battle tonight is really going to have to work for it," she predicted. Her seriousness made Romeo take in her words. He realized he had no idea who he was up against.

In a few minutes, he'd find out.

When Gary, Jodi, and Louis got to Club Limit, they found a line around the block. But they'd arrived too late — the battle had already started. If they didn't jump the line, they'd miss Romeo completely.

Failure was *not* an option.

Louis and Gary decided Jodi should be the one to approach Loshe, the club owner. Taking a break from being the emcee, Loshe stood in front of the red velvet rope and looked at the long row of fans desperate to get into the show. He smiled, satisfied.

Jodi smoothed her blue, crushed-velvet jacket and approached him. They had to see the battle tonight, and she was willing to try anything. "Has anyone ever told you that, in the right light, you look like Brad Pitt?" she asked the club owner.

Loshe didn't even look at her. "Back of the line with everyone else," he said in a bored voice. He stood planted in front of the door with folded arms.

Louis whispered to Jodi, "Try someone else."

Jodi didn't budge. She turned back to Loshe. "How about Lenny Kravitz?" she tried. She batted her eyelashes flirtatiously.

This time, Loshe gave her a weary look. Defeated, Jodi turned and slunk back to her little brother. *Time to try Plan Two*, she thought. "Gary," she whispered. "Hit it."

Gary came up to Loshe and immediately started to bawl.

"Awwwwwwwwww!!!" he sobbed. "I wanna see my brother!!" To the line of people waiting, he howled, "He won't let me iiiiiinnnnnn!" Gary pointed at Loshe and turned on the tears.

Loshe's face darkened. "Keep it down, will ya?" he said, looking nervous.

Gary cried harder. "Waaaaaahhhhhh!" he wailed.

Jodi smiled sweetly at Loshe. "He can go all night," she explained.

The people in line began to get annoyed. After a groundswell of protest, some of the club-goers started to chant, "LET HIM IN." When the entire line joined the chorus, Loshe finally relented.

"Alright," he said irritably, nodding to a huge bouncer, dressed entirely in black. The man unhooked the red velvet rope and the three kids walked in.

Gary stopped crying abruptly, and passed Loshe with a cheery smile and a wave. "Thank you," he said brightly. Louis and Jodi followed, sighing with relief. They didn't want to miss Romeo's performance.

Loshe watched them enter, then resumed his post. Romeo's family wanted to see him perform, but would they enjoy watching him demolished by Lo Key? Loshe smiled to himself. The two rappers were going to have a nasty battle, he thought, licking his lips.

He couldn't wait.

*　　*　　*

Backstage, Ro sat on a busted couch, looking over paper scraps with rhymes scrawled on them. "Raps to riches/Story of my life," he read. Not quite right, he decided. He crossed out the last line. "Raps to riches," he began again.

His concentration was shattered by Jodi's voice. "You've got exactly five seconds to explain yourself," she said grimly. Romeo looked up and saw Jodi standing in front of him, arms folded tightly across her chest. Louis and Gary flanked her on either side, eyes blazing.

He couldn't believe it.

Jodi began to count out loud. "Five, four, three, two . . ."

Romeo was dumbfounded. "What are you all doing here?" he asked in astonishment.

Just then, Myra came by waving her camera. "Great," she said. "Family picture. Smile." Before they could protest, she snapped a picture of the Miller gang: Jodi furious, Louis frowning, Gary pouting, Romeo dazed. *A real Kodak moment*, thought Romeo.

Jodi continued her rant. "I'll ask the questions," she snapped.

Gary stepped up, unable to contain himself. "Why are you leaving the band?" he wailed.

Shaking with anger, Jodi said to Romeo, "You think you can just get up and go without telling us?" she asked. The three of them looked like they were about to burst into tears.

Romeo buried his head in his hands. The night had turned into a disaster, and it had barely started. He looked at his watch. He was due on stage in five minutes.

CHAPTER 13

JUST CHOKING

Loshe squinted under the stage lights. The crowd was restless and bloodthirsty, hungry for a showdown. The noise in the room was building along with the tension. He held up a hand to control the crowd.

"Alright, alright," Loshe said, rubbing his hands together. "Things are heatin' up. Next let's bring up Mikey Mic, and the one you've been waiting for, Lo Key!"

The crowd burst into cheers. Mikey Mic was a popular rapper, known for his animated raps and goofy dance moves. The crowd itched to see him and Fan in the ring together.

Backstage, Myra turned to her cousin, Melissa. "He announced your name!" she said. "Good luck." Romeo looked up and saw Melissa head to the stage.

Myra giggled and snapped a photo of Ro's shocked face.

"Your cousin is Lo Key?" he asked, stunned.

Myra smiled even wider. "Uh-huh," she said, lifting her chin.

Ro rubbed his eyes. "Why didn't you tell me?" he asked. He never imagined Lo Key was a girl. And not just any girl — Melissa!

"I don't know," said Myra with a shrug. "She asked me not to. Plus, it's fun to see you dealing with the unexpected. I'm gonna go check her." Myra walked off toward the stage, clutching her camera.

Ro headed toward the curtain, dazed. First his family shows up, then he finds out Myra's cousin is Lo Key. Ro looked up at the ceiling. How much worse could this night get?

By the time Lo Key reached the mike, the crowd was already stoked. Myra stood in the front row, snapping photographs of her cousin. She loved watching Melissa change from a shy freshman into a glamorous rap diva.

With her masses of red hair and her silver

jacket, Melissa looked radiant. A gleaming lip stud caught the bright lights, and her bare knees poked through shredded blue jeans. The crowd was already cheering, and she hadn't said a word. Melissa took it all in. She felt like she owned the place.

Smoothing back her hair, she picked up the mike.

"Did you dream of me
Dream to have
Skills like me
If you pray every day
It's to rap like me
Act like me
Because you can't attack *like me*
Take a backseat, player. . . ."

The crowd went nuts. Myra cheered along with them, begging for more. Her cousin was on fire tonight. Mikey Mic had disappeared from sight. Having won the round meant she'd be in the final battle.

"That's what I'm talking 'bout," said Loshe, admiringly. "Lo Key moves up against . . ." He checked his list. "Romeo."

Myra smiled. This was the moment she'd been waiting for.

Romeo peeked at Lo Key through the curtain backstage. He was still absorbing the fact that his competition was Myra's cousin — and female. It put a whole new spin on the battle.

Jodi saw Romeo's distress. "This should be fun," she said. "Watching you on your own."

Romeo shook his head. "She's great," he said. His heart began to pound. "I don't know," he said, flooded with doubt.

"You don't know what?" Jodi snapped. "If you can just leave the group and go solo?"

Romeo turned away from the curtain and looked at each of them. "Jodi, Gary, Louis . . . it's not like that." He had to make them understand, but he had to go on stage. The timing couldn't have been worse.

"Then why didn't you tell us about this battle?" asked Gary.

Romeo sighed. "I heard about Lo Key and wanted to see how I could do against a rapper with a rep." Jodi rolled her eyes. "I mean it," said Ro. "This is just a way for me to make sure I've got what it takes." He paused for a moment. "'Cuz I'm sure of you guys."

Jodi, Gary, and Lou all looked at each other, then looked back at Romeo.

His eyes pleaded with them to understand. Instead of lying about the battle, he should have told them about it from the beginning, trusting they'd be cool with it. Now they felt hurt and betrayed, and there was no way to convince them otherwise.

Louis and Jodi traded glances. Romeo stuffed the scraps of paper back into his pockets. His mouth was dry and he had a headache. He opened the curtain and was blinded by the bright lights.

Meanwhile, Loshe had grabbed the mike again. "Ladies and gentlemen, in the final round, to crown our champion . . . it'll be Lo Key versus Romeo," he announced proudly. "And since this is our final battle — our two rappers can choose their own DJs. Let's hear it for Romeo!"

The crowd roared. They wanted action.

Ro hit the stage, leaving his family there to think

about what he'd just said. Sweating and unsure of himself, he walked without his usual swagger.

"Alright. Romeo, call it," said Loshe, flipping a coin.

"Heads," said Romeo, in a small voice.

"Heads it is," said Loshe, slapping the coin on his arm. "Your call."

Romeo held out his hand like a gentleman. "Ladies first," he said, trembling. Loshe handed the mike to Lo Key. A smooth groove began, and the audience started to wave their arms to the beat. Melissa nodded along for a few moments, and started her rap.

"With his Converse tied real tight he might
Just be my boy always for all days
The first boy I've known to get straight As
And appear in every one of my high school plays
Mozart blastin' from his Volvo
And there's tape on his glasses
In charge of hall passes
Not the kinda guy I mostly been with
I go for tough or Abercrombie and Fitch

With a little bit of skater boy
Here and there
Not a guy who doesn't even
Show his underwear . . ."

Romeo nodded along with the music. She was really good. Her rhymes were punctuated with salutes, pointing, dance moves — anything to make her point. He was impressed.

". . . When he sags his pants
But I wanna go with him
To the school dance and have him be my date
But I'm afraid that he doesn't know how
To move and everybody would flip and have a cow
Now just because he brings his lunch packed
This situation that I'm facing is jacked
I wouldn't call him fly, suspenders and a bow tie
I wouldn't call him the man
— But I can still be his fan."

The crowd went crazy, filling the room with shouts, cheers, and whistles. People chanted "Lo

Key!" and stomped their feet. Lo Key took a bow, flashing a curtain of dark red hair. The club seemed to explode with energy.

Loshe wiped his forehead. "Whoooooo!" he hooted "Baby, baby . . . the lyrical situation is out of control." He struggled to catch his breath, as though he had been the one performing.

Loshe handed the mike to Romeo, who took it uncertainly. "You bring a DJ, son?" he asked. Ro turned to Gary, who was peeking through the backstage curtain. With his arms folded, his brother looked angry. Ro knew he wouldn't budge.

"Uh, no, this guy is fine," Ro said unconvincingly. He looked back at Gary again. His brother frowned and looked away.

Ziggy, the DJ, started the beats. Romeo tested the mike. "Check one, check two, check three," but he didn't continue. Somehow, he couldn't get any more words out.

He tried again — nothing.

Backstage, the family watched him. "He's choking," said Louis, shaking his head.

"How do you know?" asked Jodi.

"I know all about choking," Louis insisted. "Trust me, he's doing it."

Jodi, Louis and Gary shared a look.

Onstage, Ro stood paralyzed, while the crowd yelled "CHOKE!" For what seemed like hours, he stood planted onstage, unable to move.

Loshe held his hand up to stop the booing. Romeo looked at the crowd and then down at his feet. Loshe turned to Ro. "Let's go, youngster," he ordered sharply. "Start crackin' or start packin.'" Romeo swallowed. It was his last chance to salvage the evening.

The only problem was, he had forgotten how to speak.

CHAPTER 14

LAST CHANCE

Gary and Louis watched in agony as Romeo stumbled. "I can't take this," said Gary, wringing his hands. He had to do something. On an impulse, he bolted onto the stage, and announced to the audience, "I'm his DJ!"

Everyone watched in amazement as Gary stood onstage and jumped up and down, pumping up the crowd with clenched fists. "Yeah, yeah, YEAH!" he yelled at the top of his lungs. The crowd cheered him on, enjoying his antics.

Ro turned to Gary, and smiled at him gratefully. Gary slapped his brother on the back and whispered, "C'mon, Ro, you can do it." He motioned for the other DJ to leave. Sitting down at the console, Gary started dropping his beats.

Jodi and Louis burst onto the stage next, flashing Ro a smile and a thumbs-up. "C'mon, bro," added Louis, squeezing his shoulder. "We're here for you, Ro," said Jodi, swaying to the music.

Taking their place alongside Gary, Jodi and Louis prepared to give Romeo backup. *It's just like we're doing a concert*, Jodi tried to tell herself. She tried not to be rattled by the impatient crowd.

Romeo swallowed and took the mike back, not sure if he could force any words out. But Gary's beats were irresistible, and he could feel himself drawn in to the luscious groove. People began waving their arms over their heads again. The place was rocking — all they needed was a singer.

Romeo stepped up, and the rhymes took over.

"They can't stop us, right you know
They can't stop us
All the things y'all did, man, we done did that
All the things y'all wish for
We didn't have that
All the new things that's not even out yet
Guess what, me and my crew we got

That we knew no limit y'all
Should know that
Won't stop, can't stop
Y'all should know that."

Again, Romeo felt himself feeding off the crowd's energy. He and the audience were one now, rocking the mic something fierce. His voice rose and he took the music up to a whole new level.

"We was born to ball, that's how we livin'
Ain't no faking or no gimmicks
We work hard, that's why we winnin'
They can't stop us, them boys over there
They can't stop us, them girls over there
They can't stop us, them boys over there
They can't stop us
They can't stop us right."

The crowd let loose a series of wild cheers. Whistles, foot-stomping, and clapping followed. Sweat poured down Romeo's face, but he was smiling at Louis, Jodi, and Gary. He'd done it.

Even though the music had stopped, Louis was still grooving wildly, clapping his hands above his head. His brothers and sister looked at him.

"Louis, you alright?" asked Gary, shaking him. "Louis?"

But Louis was somewhere else, tapping into the waves of energy that flowed all around him. "Yeah, I'm cool," he said, his eyes lighting up. "And I just found my thing. Watch!"

At that moment, Louis leaped off the stage and dove shoulder-first into the audience. He sailed off the stage with complete confidence, arms spread like wings. The crowd caught him with arms outstretched and passed him around. With hands out to his sides, Louis collected high fives.

"Whoa!" said Gary. "What the . . . ?"

Myra spun around to see him. "I think he's lost his mind," she said, to no one in particular. She snapped a picture. It wasn't every day you saw your friends being handled like a human Frisbee.

As he got tossed from one person to another, Louis was having the time of his life. He crisscrossed the room on his stomach, cheered on by the crowd.

His body-surfing stunt took the party up an extra notch.

Loshe waited for the noise to die down. "Good job, rookie," he said to Romeo, patting him on the back. Pointing to the audience, he said, "Now, let's hear what they all think."

Facing the crowd, he said, "Give it up for Romeo." People cheered, waved their arms, and shouted. Romeo smiled, looking down at his black sneakers. Could he dare to hope that he'd won?

Loshe gestured toward Melissa, as if bowing to a queen. "And, of course, the undefeated Lo Key." People cheered even louder — this time, the noise was deafening. For several minutes, the crowd brought down the house with their screams and whooping.

It was obvious that Lo Key was the people's choice.

Loshe turned to Melissa, lifting her hand as if she were a boxing champ. "And it looks like Lo Key is still the reigning winner." The red-headed rapper opened her arms wide and took a bow. She straightened her jacket, and the crowd erupted once more in thunderous applause.

Ro clapped hard. He was disappointed that he had lost but relieved that he'd managed to turn things around after he'd choked. His family gathered around to give him hugs.

"That's okay, Ro," said Gary.

Jodi mussed his hair. "You did great," she said, meaning it.

Ro's family was proud of him for taking the challenge, and surviving. He'd overcome his panic and made a strong showing against a fierce opponent. Against all odds, he'd pulled through.

As far as Ro was concerned, it was his family who had saved him. Seeing them appear onstage, he'd never been so grateful for their support. When he had looked in their eyes, he saw their faith in him, and he knew he could do it.

Outside the club, Melissa and Myra came up to Ro. With her hair in a scarf, and a backpack slung over her shoulder, Melissa looked less like a rap diva. She touched Romeo's shoulder. "No hard feelings, I hope," she said.

Romeo smiled. "Hey, I'd rather get floored by the best than sweep up the rest." He and Melissa touched fists. Besides being an awesome rapper, she seemed cool. He hoped to get to know her.

"Nice," said Myra, looking at her cousin and smiling.

Melissa chuckled. "You should get that one down for your rhyme book," she said to Romeo. "Use it in your next rap."

Ro pulled scraps of paper from his pockets to show them. "Already got it down," he said. "Seriously, it was great to battle a first-rate rapper," said Romeo. "You really lived up to your rep."

Melissa smiled, touched. "You're pretty awesome yourself," she said. "Myra said you'd tear up the place." Myra blushed and fiddled with her camera.

"C'mon, cousin, your fans are waiting," said Myra, leading her cousin over to a crowd of people. Romeo waved as he watched Myra and Melissa walk away.

Jodi, Louis, and Gary came up next, smothering Ro again with hugs and high fives.

"Ro," Louis hailed him.

"You got skills, bro," said Jodi.

Gary playfully punched him in the stomach. "Thanks," Ro said, pretending to be knocked out.

Even Loshe came by to shake his hand. "You got it goin' on, junior," said the club owner. "It looked touch and go for a while, but in the end, you really pulled it out," he said. "I hope you'll come back to Club Limit for the next battle."

Before Ro could answer, a sleek silver Jaguar pulled up next to them. Inside was a hip-looking, olive-skinned man with a goatee. He pulled off aviator sunglasses and leaned out the window. "Romeo Miller?" he said.

Romeo spun around. "Yeah?" he answered. Loshe took off.

"I've been all over looking for you," the man said.

What now? thought Ro. After his roller coaster of a night, he wasn't up for more surprises.

But he had a feeling he was about to get one.

CHAPTER 15

BIG DEAL

The man handed him a business card. "I'm Jive Rivera. Heirloom Records," he said. "You're good, man."

Romeo nodded, surprised. Heirloom was a hot label. Some major Seattle R&B acts had recorded with them. They were known for scouting out promising local talent. "Thanks, thanks a lot," he repeated.

Jive looked Romeo up and down. "No, you're *real* good," he said. "I saw the battle, and you knocked 'em out." He turned off the engine of the car and leaned on the window. "You knocked *me* out."

Romeo zipped and unzipped his sweatshirt nervously. "Thanks," he said.

Jive opened the car door, and stretched out his legs. "What would you say to a deal with Heirloom?"

As he said this, he hooked the sunglasses over his black T-shirt.

A deal with Heirloom? Was this guy for real? Ro had been waiting for this moment his whole life. Romeo wanted to throw up his hat and jump for joy.

Instead, he looked at his family. They looked back at him uncertainly. "I'd say that sounds great, but . . ." He walked over to his siblings and put his arm around Gary. "When you ask me something, you gotta ask *them* something. My family. Our band. The Romeo Show."

Jive shrugged. "Alright. What do you and your family say to a record deal?"

Jodi, Louis, and Gary all looked at each other. A recording deal for all of them? They couldn't believe their ears. Jodi signaled a thumps-up to Romeo, and Louis and Gary nodded vigorously.

"Cool," said Jive. "I'll be in touch."

Louis turned to Jodi and mouthed, "It's awesome," and Gary squealed. Jodi stifled her excitement and whispered to her brothers, "Calm down!" She wanted them to look cool in front of Jive — as though getting a recording deal was an everyday occurrence. She gave a prim wave.

Romeo took her cue and acted businesslike. "Okay, you can reach our manager, Hacksaw Hacklinburg. He's the one to talk to," he said, patting the body of the silver Jaguar. *Sweet car*, he thought.

"Great, I know the guy," said Jive. "We'll speak soon." He got back into his car, made a peace sign with his fingers, and drove off.

The moment he pulled away, Jodi screamed. "Yessssssss!" she yelled. Romeo and she high-fived with gusto. Louis and Gary collided in a massive chest bump.

Ro picked up Gary and spun him around on his shoulders. Jodi threw her purse in the air. The four of them locked arms in a mad "happy dance" around the parking lot. They hammed it up with spins, shoulder rolls, and body ripples. Louis kept punching his fist in the air.

They had been offered a recording deal! And best of all, the band had made it on their own. They hadn't had to rely on their record-producer dad to get them into the business. Percy Miller would be proud of them.

People streaming out of the club looked at the

four kids clowning and hugging each other. The bouncer smiled at them, and asked if they could move to the side. They kept dancing, barely hearing him.

Ro looked up at the sky thoughtfully. In one night he had gone from the depths of despair to walking on clouds. His wildest dreams had come true. He fingered the card in his pocket, outlining the raised letters that spelled out "Heirloom."

He looked at his family again, dancing and celebrating. He couldn't think of anyone he'd rather share it with.

The next night, the family gathered around the dinner table. Angeline had baked a cake frosted to look like an old 45 record. Their father was coming home late from a business trip, and would be home any minute. They couldn't wait to tell him about their recording deal.

Angeline begged them to tell the story again. "So you found out about the rap battle because I cleaned up the boys' bedroom?" she asked.

Jodi started over. "When you found the flyer, we realized where Romeo had been going all this time." She turned to her brother. "The library! That was a good one."

Romeo looked sheepish. "I had to say *something*," he offered. "I pretended I had a biology test."

"Then you said it was a history test," said Jodi. "When I busted you, you said it was the history of biology. Yeah, right," she rolled her eyes.

"I thought he had suddenly turned into this serious student," said Louis. "Missing music rehearsal to study. Either that, or he had met some girl," he said, balling up his napkin and throwing it at Ro.

"I should've told y'all where I was going. I just didn't think. It was easier to just make up some story," he said. "I needed to do it on my own. Just to see if I could."

Jodi explained how once they learned about the battle, they dashed over to Club Limit — only to find they couldn't get in. "That's where Gary came in," she said proudly. Gary pretended to tear up, then smiled. "What can I say?" he said. "I got skills."

Angeline warned him not to try any phony waterworks at home. Gary said he wasn't sure he could top that performance anyway. Louis joked that if they'd had a crying battle, Gary would have won hands down.

Romeo described being on the couch backstage, looking up from his rhymes to see his family glaring at him. "I was, like, not now, y'all — I got a battle to do."

Discovering Myra's cousin was another shock. "Here's this girl I've met at school, through Myra. All of a sudden, they announce Lo Key, and out she walks," Romeo marveled. "I was, like, HUH?"

"Your face was practically gray, man," chuckled Louis. "I thought you were gonna lose it."

Angeline asked, "Why is battling a girl such a big deal?"

Ro tried to explain. "I just thought it would be some big guy bragging about his coolness. The first two guys I battled were kind of like that," he recalled. "Having a girl there really threw me off."

It was also unsettling to learn his opponent was someone he knew, he thought. When they first met, he remembered telling her what it was like to "be in the flow," as if she wouldn't know anything about being onstage. Thinking about that made him wince.

"She turned out to be a really great rapper,

though," said Romeo. "Competing with her brought my game to a new level." Her verbal creativity had made him think about rapping in a fresh way. Instead of trying to be tough, she had told a funny story about herself.

Louis produced a photo of Romeo and Melissa before the show, looking like they belonged to the same crew. He said, "Myra sent this today, and I printed it out to show you." It was taken before Romeo knew Fan's identity.

Gary jumped up and imitated Lo Key. "My boyfriend has a calculator and bow tie/Chess club or not, I still think he's fly," he sang in a high voice. Angeline and Louis started throwing paper cups at him.

"Hey, that sounds like someone I would like," protested Jodi.

Romeo grabbed a spoon and started to use it as a mike. "Ummmm . . . what do I do, y'all?" he stammered, acting out the moment he panicked. He stood on a chair for extra impact. "Ayyyyyyyyyyyyy . . ." he said, tipping the chair.

Louis cupped his mouth and chanted, "CHOKE," imitating the audience.

Just then, the front door opened and Percy Miller walked in. He looked at Romeo, standing on a chair and stuttering into a spoon. "What in the world . . . ?" he said. Angeline shrugged, and the kids cracked up.

He put down his black briefcase and looked at the record-shaped cake. Walking over to the table, he dipped into the blue frosting and licked his finger. "Is there something I should know about?" he asked, looking from person to person.

"It's a long story," Jodi said. "We can't wait to tell you ALL about it."

THE END